RIVERDALE

DEATH OF A CHEERLEADER

RIVERDALE

DEATH OF A CHEERLEADER

An original novel by Micol Ostow

SCHOLASTIC LTD.

Published in the UK by Scholastic Children's Books, 2020
Euston House, 24 Eversholt Street, London, NW1 1DB
A division of Scholastic Limited

London ~ New York ~ Toronto ~ Sydney ~ Auckland
Mexico City ~ New Delhi ~ Hong Kong

SCHOLASTIC and associated logos are trademarks and/or
registered trademarks of Scholastic Inc.

First published in the US by Scholastic Inc., 2020

© 2020 Archie Comics Publications, Inc.

ISBN 978 0702 30076 9

A CIP catalogue record for this book is available from the British
Library.

All rights reserved.
This book is sold subject to the condition that it shall not, by way of
trade or otherwise, be lent, hired out or otherwise circulated in any
form of binding or cover other than that in which it is published. No
part of this publication may be reproduced, stored in a retrieval
system, or transmitted in any form or by any other means (electronic,
mechanical, photocopying, recording or otherwise) without prior
written permission of Scholastic Limited.

This book is a work of fiction. Names, characters, places and incidents
are either the product of the author's imagination or are used
fictitiously, and any resemblance to actual persons, living or dead,
business establishments, events or locales is entirely coincidental.

Printed by CPI Group (UK) Ltd, Croydon, CR0 4YY
Papers used by Scholastic Children's Books are made from
wood grown in sustainable forests.

2 4 6 8 10 9 7 5 3 1

Book design by Jessica Meltzer

PROLOGUE

JUGHEAD

Riverdale is a small town, dripping with "quaint." It's easy for the casual observer to assume that life here is nothing but homespun charm and down-home values, whatever that even means. But if you know this place, you know how utterly deceiving looks can be. Think less *American*, heavy on the *Gothic*, and you're on the right track. And what we now know with unwavering certainty? In this town, there is no rest, nor a modicum of relief, for the weary.

One other adage that we all know well? *"Nothing gold can stay."*

Though I hadn't read *The Outsiders* since middle school, I'd never been more aware of that poignant quote than I was the fall we kicked off our senior year at Riverdale High. Truly, though, nothing gold *could* stay; it never does. And nowhere was that fact truer than in our deceptive little town, where the only constant was change, and the only reliable fact was the presence of uncertainty, of chaos.

Some philosophers extol the virtues of change, loudly proclaiming how instability forces us, as a species, to evolve. But in our not-so-sleepy hamlet, those who were the primary agents of change were less about virtue and more about . . .

Well, the seven deadly sins come to mind.

This eternal flux of change extended itself to every banal facet of Riverdale life. Our first case in point: Technically, I wasn't even *at* Riverdale High. Not anymore.

For senior year, I had left Riverdale High in a thick roar of my motorcycle's engine, a cloud of smoke curling from the exhaust pipe as I cruised out of town to tiny Stonewall Prep boarding school. In a word, it was *unexpected*.

The last time I'd left Riverdale, it was begrudgingly, under duress; I was shuttled to Southside High after first being cycled into foster care. To be fair, it wasn't a terrible experience—at Southside, I had found a place with my people, the Serpents. And for the first time in my life, I allowed myself to embrace my legacy with them. (Lately, we'd even grown our numbers with an informal alliance with Toni Topaz's Pretty Poisons.)

This time, I was leaving Riverdale High by choice. Even if it *was* a difficult one—with consequences, both anticipated and unforeseen. The opportunity to enroll at Stonewall Prep had presented itself to me, practically unbidden. It was a shiny brass ring on a carnival carousel, and I'd grabbed it with both hands, tight.

Because admission to Stonewall meant that I might have a shot at leaving behind a legacy, too: by following my dream of becoming a writer. Stonewall gave me a chance to go somewhere that nurtured my work and encouraged me to take it seriously. It physically pained me to leave my friends behind—to say nothing of what it felt like to be separated from Betty—but this was a step toward a larger plan, a path to becoming the first in my family to go to college.

Nothing gold could stay—but greener pastures? They were out there, once in the rarest of whiles, if you were willing to go out on a limb.

That's why they're called *hard* choices, right? Because they're hard. And they have repercussions. I tried to stay positive, to expect the best, even if I wasn't a shiny-happy enough guy to flat-out *hope* for it. If I believed in anything in this bizarre, unpredictable world, I had to allow myself—however naïvely, I'll admit—to believe that Betty and I were unbreakable.

But only time would tell; we both knew that. And even though we weren't admitting it out loud or in so many words, I knew we were both at least a little bit worried, too. (Maybe *more* than a little bit—though if you asked me straight-up I'd deny it with everything I've got.)

Of course, Betty was fully supportive of my decision to enroll at Stonewall. She understood the unbelievable opportunity it was for me. But the idea of being physically separated for days or weeks at a time? How could we *not* have nagging doubts?

It wasn't only us, after all. Transition—with everything fraught and complicated that it implicitly carried—was a virus burning through our town's bloodstream. Call it something in the air. Some uniquely Riverdale quality that insists on consuming and annihilating anything good, pure, reliable, or stable in its path.

Varchie, for instance, was dealing with their own unbearable strain right now, too. Archie had been through a veritable wringer last year, but he had managed to come out the other side through sheer force of will. This, in addition to his friends' support, of course. And Veronica was the first one in his corner every time, no question.

Now, the less straightforward question—for any of us who loved Archie as much as we did—was how to help our boy get through the devastating loss of his father. Fred Andrews's absence was one we all felt acutely. There was nothing to say or to do to lessen our friend's pain. But Veronica was determined to try. We all were.

In typical Archie fashion, he was putting on a brave face: converting the El Royale boxing gym into a community center in his father's honor, looking out for neighborhood kids who might be in need of a Good Samaritan, just the way his father would have. The way his father always did.

I think all three of us worried that, to some extent, he was trying to keep busy, to distract himself. There was nothing wrong with that, especially not if it was what he needed to cope. I know, though, that we all wanted him to feel like he could open up to us. We wanted to be there for him, to comfort him. But the rest was up to Archie—no matter how hard it was for us to just stand by and watch while he struggled. Especially given that we were dealing with our own struggles, too.

For me, specifically, that meant the Stonewall Four.

Four students, presumed "missing." Regardless of how insignificant, how deeply insufficient, that term was. Had I honestly thought I would transfer schools and escape my hometown scot-free? Chaos, loss, and confusion, they clung to me, nipping at my heels. You could take the boy out of Riverdale, but there was no taking the Riverdale out of the boy.

Which meant that any hopes my friends and I had of quietly becoming "normal high school students" just in time for senior year were long gone, well buried. That pipe dream of "being seventeen" in its most innocent incarnation had been relegated to a drawer, dashed by the very same forces that failed to keep the shadows at bay even from events as mainstream, as benign, as a school play.

We were, quite possibly, doomed.

And yet, some part of us must have still had fleeting hope in a secret corner of our hearts. Hope that there was still a chance, that things could be different. Better. I had *left*, after all. I was at Stonewall Prep now, taking a step toward rewriting the script of the film noir I'd unwittingly been born into.

I'd left for Stonewall, and Betty and I were doing our damnedest to err toward distance making the heart grow fonder. And Veronica was watching, ever optimistic, as Archie tried to rebuild the cornerstones of his world.

We were doing our best.

Admittedly, to middling results. No matter how ardently we threw ourselves into these so-called normal pursuits—a guys poker night, a cheerleading retreat, the stuff of teen TV dramas—the insidious, essential Riverdaleness of it all kept creeping back in.

How did that saying go?

Oh, right: *"The definition of insanity is doing the same thing over and over again, and expecting a different result."*

Still, here we were, senior year, trying *yet again* to be better, to be different, to dream bigger. To dare to imagine a world beyond the horror and destruction, the callow dysfunction of Riverdale. Of fate.

I didn't want to think we were insane. So, if it wasn't insanity driving us . . .? "Hope" was the only conclusion left to draw.

We hoped even in the face of overwhelmingly discouraging experiences. Even in the absence of any real reason to feel anything more than cautious optimism. Another saying: "Hope springs eternal." And my friends and I were turning out to be proof positive of just that.

Come to think of it: Maybe that *was* insanity, after all.

PART ONE:
THE BEST-LAID PLANS

CHAPTER ONE

☀ RIVW WEATHER   1 min. ago

A severe weather advisory is in effect for Riverdale and the
surrounding townships from now through Sunday evening.
Meteorologists are predicting heavy rains and gale-force winds,
with the possibility of flash floods arising quickly. Please tune in
for ongoing coverage and further updates. We care about your
safety!

—RIVW.com and affiliates

ᴧᴧᴧ

Veronica:

Good morning, Archiekins! How's my favorite early bird?

Archie:

Hey, Ronnie! I'm OK. Tired. I was up late
cleaning up at the community center.

Veronica:

Those kids are so lucky to have you.

Archie:

I guess . . . I just wish I could do more.

Archie:

Sorry, I'm being a downer. Long story short: I'm good. So, what's up?

Veronica:

My stalwart Red Paladin. I hope you know it's OK if you're not good.

Veronica:

You've had a time of it. And you can and should be processing in your own way, on your own schedule. You needn't put on a brave face for me.

Archie:

I know, Ronnie. You've been amazing since everything with my dad. You have no idea how much I appreciate it.

Veronica:

Well, as you said yourself: I only wish I could do more.

Veronica:

In the meantime, though, woefully inadequate though it may be, I do have a suggestion, hopefully more appealing than catching the proverbial worm.

Veronica:

I'm meeting Betty at Pop's for a little pre-school day sustenance. How about you come, too? I know she'd love to see you. Plus, it's been too long since we just kicked back like regular high schoolers enjoying some much-earned senioritis.

Archie:

Yeah, I guess it has. And I wish I could. It would be nice to feel normal again.

Veronica:

But you're busy?

Archie:

I am, yeah.

Veronica:

Surely the community center is immaculate?

Archie:

It is, but there are a million other things I need to take care of there. You know how it is, you've got La Bonne Nuit.

Archie:

And with Dad gone . . . I'm trying to keep an eye on Andrews Construction, too—all the lumber deliveries and stuff. Just, you know, until we find someone to take over the logistics for the construction crew. And there are a ton of deliveries this morning.

Veronica:

Got it. I do know how it goes. And, obvi, I think you're amazing for keeping the community center AND the construction business running smoothly. I know your dad would be so proud of you. Just like I am.

Archie:

I hope so. I mean, I'm trying.

Veronica:

You're SUCCEEDING, Archie. I repeat: You. Are. AMAZING.

Veronica:

But you don't have to be amazing all on your own. Is there ANYTHING I can do to help? I'm pretty great at logistics, if I do say so myself. Let me lighten your load. Isn't that what best girls are for?

Veronica:

It'd be a true shame if we let all my Pop's and La Bonne Nuit management experience go to waste . . .

Archie:

No!

Archie:

I mean, yes, you're super experienced. And that's so sweet. YOU are amazing, too, of course. But I'm good.

Veronica:

You've got a support system, Archiekins. People who are here for you, who WANT you to lean on them.

Archie:

I know. But my mom is on top of everything right now. All the manager stuff. So I don't need to burden you with any of that.

Veronica:

It's not a burden, Archie. Don't ever think that. I'm here, anytime, day or night. Just say the word and let me know if—and when—there's ANYTHING I can do.

Archie:

I will. And thanks. But you really don't have to worry about me, Ronnie. I swear.

Veronica:

I can't help it, Archie. But I'll take you at your word.

Archie:

Cool. Well . . . I guess I'll see you at school?

Veronica:

Absolutely. ☺

∿∿∿

BETTY

Of all the drama unfolding in Riverdale of late, you could probably argue that relationship stuff fell pretty low on the priority list. Jughead and I doing the long-distance thing? That paled in comparison to the revelations that—oh, just as a fun for instance—*my own mother* had been a sleeper agent working with the FBI to take down an organ-harvesting cult . . . And that my long-lost (then found, then lost *again*) half brother—who was *my boyfriend's half brother, too*—was running the whole sting the entire time.

And that was just the tip of the iceberg around here. You'd think we'd be used to it, that we'd have learned to take it all in stride by now. But I guess there are just some things that manage to totally pull the rug out from under you every time . . .

Here, under the jaundiced hum of Pop's fluorescent lighting, the simple look on Veronica's face said it all. And that was even *before* she'd filled me in on every last excruciating detail of her exchange with Archie over our crack-of-dawn cheese omelets while I did my best not to visibly react.

"A *smiley face emoji*! B, what have I come to?" Veronica cringed and took a sip from her steaming coffee mug. "Is there a handbook somewhere? Some step-by-step, detailed guide to helping one's significant other through the death of a loved one, do you think? Because if so, let's see if Glamazon will deliver it two-day shipping. I'm drowning, girl." She paused, reconsidering. "Or, rather, *Archie's* drowning. And I want, more than anything, to throw him a lifeline." Her eyes welled with tears. "But I just can't figure out *how*."

I gave her a supportive smile. "I'm sure you're doing better than you're giving yourself credit for. As for the handbook . . ." I shrugged. "We can Google, after school. I mean, there's *got* to be something out there that's useful."

"I *hope* so. I'd like to believe I have something to offer

Archie by way of actual, real comfort or emotional strength. And some days, I manage to convince myself that I do. That I'm helping him through this . . . impossible gauntlet of grief. But then . . ." She sighed, trailing off.

"But then, awkwardly peppy *smiley face emoji*," I said, giving Veronica my best sympathetic look. It wasn't much of a stretch for me to imagine how my best friend was feeling right now, given that I'd had so many weird, similarly stilted exchanges with Jughead lately. "I'm familiar with that situation myself."

I mean—Jughead's mother had come back to town from her first unexpected walkabout, only to take over the local drug trade right behind her own family's back. And then she bailed on said family all over again. There were no words I could say to make Jughead feel less abandoned. There was no way to convince him of how wholly and thoroughly loved he was—*is*. Believe me, I'd tried.

Veronica stabbed at a bite of egg, then pushed it aside on her plate. "Equal weirdness with Jughead, huh?"

I gave her a wry grin. "Oh yes. One hundred percent. Although, I'm trying not to be too possessive of his time, even though I'm obviously totally freaking out that we're separated while he's at Stonewall. It was bad enough when he was at Southside High. Now he's *boarding* at a fancy private school in another town?"

"Only on weekdays. And, as they say . . . distance makes

the heart grow fonder," Veronica pointed out, raising an eyebrow.

"Counterpoint: Out of sight, out of mind." Now it was my turn to sigh. "I keep trying to remind myself that this isn't, like, the end of the world. Stonewall is an *amazing* opportunity for Jug, and he had to take it. And as for being wrapped up in his sister's life when he's home . . . I mean, I'd have to be a monster to be jealous of that."

"And yet."

"And yet." I set my utensils down on my plate, giving up on eating for good. "I'll admit it—I want him all to myself!" I sighed. "Don't listen to me; I'm being awful. Trust me, I know it's *good* that he's looking out for JB now that Gladys is gone. He wouldn't be the Jughead I love if he *weren't* so worried about her. I mean, for starters, JB needs the attention—I'm sure she's feeling totally abandoned." I leaned in, elbows on the table, careful to avoid a tiny patch of dried maple syrup left over from someone else's meal.

Veronica nodded. "Well, real talk: She kind of *was*. So, yeah."

"But the truth is . . . I think *Jug* needs it, too." I paused. "I know he likes to pretend he's so stoic—total disaffected youth, nothing ever gets him, you know—"

"I *do* know," Veronica agreed.

"But, well . . . he's not a *robot*. He's a teenager, with feelings. Whose mom has now walked out on him twice. And he won't talk about it. He wants to be all strong. For me, for JB . . ."

Veronica huffed. "What is it with these boys and their out-dated notions of stolid invulnerability?"

"Don't ask me. I'll admit, it stings a little. But even if he doesn't want to show it, I know he's hurting. So I think . . . I think it's good for him to have JB to look after. Even if that means there's less time left for me."

"Misery loves company," Veronica offered.

Misery. That was the word for it. "For one, yeah . . . but more than that, even . . . I think it gives him a sense of . . . I don't know, purpose? Does that make sense?"

"Absolutely," Veronica said, considering her breakfast one last time before pushing her plate aside entirely like I had. "It's probably not that different from Archie, running in circles, staying busy with the community center and keeping an eye on his dad's construction deliveries . . . He wants to be strong. But I can see the pain in those soulful eyes of his. It's not about his father's business—not really. It's that he needs to keep his father's *legacy* alive."

Her words struck a chord. Archie wasn't the only one of us who'd lost a father recently. Though my own father's legacy was one I'd be happy to see buried alongside his body.

"Can you blame him?" I asked quietly. "Fred Andrews was special."

"Beyond special. One of the most loving, loyal fathers I've ever had the honor of knowing."

I knew Veronica was thinking of her *own* father's legacy—and his extended criminal enterprise.

"I don't blame Archie one bit," she said wistfully. "I just wish there was something more I could do to actually *help* him. Comforting platitudes . . . they only go so far. To say nothing of humiliating emojis and LOLspeak."

"I know," I said, just as dejected as she was. "I really, really know."

"I know you do." She reached across the table and patted my hand. "At least you get me, girl. What would I do without my bestie to complain to, on occasion?"

"Well, you said it yourself—misery *does* love company." We both had to smile at that.

"Meanwhile," I went on, feeling suddenly slightly more cautious, "speaking of parental legacies . . ." I tilted my head at her, questioning, not wanting to say outright what I *knew* she was thinking about.

She raised an eyebrow. "Oh, you mean, how am I doing now that not one but *both* of my parents are incarcerated?"

"I hope it's okay to ask," I said, apologetic. "I mean . . . my father was the Black Hood. No judgment, obviously."

She waved a hand at me. "Obviously. And please. No secrets between us, you know that. Besides, if I didn't have you to vent to, I'd probably have gone stark raving mad by now."

"So, that means you're . . ." I prompted.

"Hanging on, even if only by the slimmest of silken threads," she said. It wasn't exactly reassuring, but then again, if I knew my V, she had inner strength to spare. Besides, for better or for worse, this wasn't her first rodeo dealing with the fallout from her parents' shadier dealings. This time, she'd even had a hand in their downfall (albeit with a predictably unpredictable outcome).

"At least with your father in jail, he's out of your hair?" I ventured. I wasn't sure that was how Hiram Lodge worked, but I'd keep my fingers crossed.

"That's the theory," Veronica said. "But we'll have to see about how—or *if*—it works that way in practice, too. Alas, it's impossible to say how long the arm of Hiram Lodge truly is— even from behind bars."

It was a sobering thought. I sat up straighter against the squishy vinyl backing of the booth. "This is unacceptable, V," I said, trying to sound authoritative. "Things may not be . . . ideal around here, these days, but it's not like *that's* anything new."

"No, we are certainly no strangers to tumult," Veronica agreed. She fished a few bills from her wallet to cover her half of our tab as Pop swung by, smiling, and delivered it, facedown, to our table.

"Shouldn't you girls be on your way to school?" he asked, friendly.

"That's the next stop," Veronica said. "We were just hoping to drown our sorrows in a splash more caffeine before we hit the road."

"Absolutely." He moved to grab the coffeepot from the burner behind the counter to refill our mugs.

"You were saying something about unacceptable," Veronica prompted, once she'd had another healthy sip of caffeinated fortification.

"I was saying we need to do something other than sit around and wallow about how helpless we are to do anything for Archie and Jughead—or any of our friends at school who are going through something right now—"

"—which is, as per usual, a *lot* of them."

"Right. I think a little brainstorming about what we could do to help them might be . . . empowering. And maybe a little self-care for us while we're at it?"

"Mmm, good call. Maybe Sunday night, after your beau has gone back to his new cloistered, *Secret History*–esque den of privilege."

I groaned. "Please don't remind me." Weekends with Jug were just not enough.

"I apologize. But you're right—a girls night with some tactical planning is just what the doctor ordered. How do you feel about organic sheet masks and a screening of *Legally Blonde* on our new home-movie system? With a side of Magnolia cupcakes driven direct from the West Village by Smithers."

"Hmm." I thought about it. "I do love a good sheet mask."

Both of our phones buzzed at once, clattering loudly on the surface of the table. Veronica grabbed hers before I could reach mine, and she peered at her screen. She swiped her finger across the screen to unlock the phone. "Hold that thought. Girls night planning may have to wait. It's Cheryl," she said. "It's an APB. A text blast to all the Vixens. We're supposed to check our email."

I made a face. "She texted us to tell us she emailed us?"

"It's *Cheryl*," Veronica repeated pointedly. "Honestly, we should probably be relieved she didn't send carrier pigeons, just for the sake of the dramatic impact."

"True." I scanned my own email. "She's saying . . . we need to be in the gym before first period."

Veronica glanced at the gleaming Swiss timepiece on her wrist. "So, basically now."

"And here we were *just* saying we needed something to do." Unfortunately, I had the sinking feeling this was the wrong kind of something.

"Next time, we'll remember the old adage," Veronica said.

"Which one?"

She grinned at me knowingly, grabbing her snakeskin Birkin and sliding it into the crook of her elbow. "'Let sleeping Vixens lie.'"

"Where Cheryl Blossom is involved?" I laughed. "Not very likely."

CHAPTER TWO

Alice Cooper:

Betty, have you seen my gold hoop earrings? The ones with the quartz?

Betty:

No, why?

Alice Cooper:

I can't find them anywhere. I have a feeling we're going to be doing a LOT of storm coverage, which means a LOT of airtime for yours truly. And those quartz stones pick up the light in the studio perfectly.

Betty:

Sorry to spoil your . . . natural disaster?

Alice Cooper:

Very funny, Elizabeth.

Betty:

Haven't seen them in a while, though. Hope you find them! Gotta run to a Vixens meeting. I'll keep an eye out! xo

~~~

FROM: Cheryl Blossom
TO: [list—all Vixens FULL]
SUBJECT: Mandatory assemblage

Greetings, cherished underlings—

It is my duty, if not necessarily my pleasure, to inform you that we Vixens will be congregating in the school gymnasium just before first period for a late-breaking announcement. If the threat of my own attendance doesn't inspire promptness, know that our new Principal Honey will be the one making said announcement. Surely that should help to hasten your stride.

Regardless, take note, my chums: This email is *not* a request but a requirement.

I'll see you all shortly.

—Cheryl

~~~

Toni:

Cher—what's the big secret announcement?

Cheryl:

Silly TeeTee—do you really think I'd give you special privileges simply because you're my paramour?

Toni:

Well, actually . . .

Cheryl:

Because if so, of course you're absolutely correct. Meet me at my locker and I'll fill you in while we walk over.

Toni:

Be there in a sec.

⌒⌒⌒

FROM: Principal Honey
TO: Cheryl Blossom
SUBJECT: Newest faculty

Good morning, Cheryl—

Coach Grappler is excited to meet our Riverdale Vixens. I trust you've contacted them and that we can expect to see everyone in the gymnasium at a quarter to first period? I'm assuming a prompt arrival. We want to give Coach Grappler our warmest Bulldog welcome!

∿∿

FROM: Cheryl Blossom
TO: Principal Honey
SUBJECT: RE: Newest faculty

I'm insulted you even had to ask, Principal Honey. My River Vixens have been briefed and summoned, and they eagerly await *this* newest addition to our Bulldog community. And speaking only for myself, I, for one, will be there with crimson bells chiming!

Fret not, Principal Honey. I won't let anything ruin this announcement. It will be nothing less than a sheer delight!

∿∿

CHERYL

"Oh, TeeTee . . . *j'adore* the scent of Elnett in the morning. It's so . . . invigorating." I took a deep breath and inhaled the sharp antiseptic bite of the technically unscented hair spray that was, apparently, the River Vixens' styling product of overwhelming choice. Funny how an unscent was somehow still perfectly detectable at no less than fifty feet.

"It does really . . . linger in the air." Toni sniffed with caution, clearly less enthralled by the buzz of energy permeating the gymnasium than I was.

Then again, that's why she was the eternal yin to my yang, the pretty to my poison (or was it the other way around?), the veritable cola to my cherry syrup. Without fail, Antoinette Topaz could be counted on to regard oncoming change with a clear and level head . . . whereas, if I'm being fully honest? Yours truly had a *tiny* tendency to leap straight into any and all fray without a second glance. Together, we were the perfect balance.

And I'd need Toni's balance today as Principal Honey prepared to drop a demibombshell of his own on my merry band. I'd assured him that the Vixens would be thrilled to greet the arrival of a new cheer coach. And, they would be . . . if they knew what was good for them.

Fortunately, the girls had taken my email missives with the appropriate gravity I'd intended; not a single one was even a moment late for our last-minute concursion. Now my whole team, blinking and beaming in equal parts enthusiasm and hesitancy, sat perched on the bleachers while they awaited the news.

Good. They could wait for a few minutes more. There is something to be said for building anticipation, after all.

From above, a throat cleared pointedly. I glanced up. Veronica Lodge, of course. A talented Vixen, and only marginally less endowed in the respective departments of brains and beauty than *moi*, but perennially a thorn in my ever-so-shapely side. While I enjoy a challenge, I did often find Veronica's fire exhausting. She tends to need reminders as to who the HBIC is around here.

(Me, always. In case you needed reminding as well.)

"Yes?" I asked, my tone challenging.

She rolled her eyes. "Cheryl, I beg you—spare us the dramatic buildup. You summoned us. We obliged. Can we just . . . get on with it?"

I waved her off. "Your enthusiasm is noted."

Another eye roll from Veronica at that.

"Of course, now that we're all gathered, I'll dive right in to our exciting news." I nodded to Tina Patel, who'd been standing at attention by the side door to the coach's interior office, and she now pulled it open.

"Principal Honey, Coach Grappler—please do come join us anon!"

A wave of murmurs broke out amid the bleachers as Honey strode out of the office with our fearless new leader in tow. Honey was smiling, a somewhat rare sight for the generally stern man. But the Vixens weren't focused on him. It was the woman beside him who had everyone all atwitter with curiosity.

Greta Grappler was a solid, formidable presence who

announced her authority with every step she took. She was as tall as an Amazon, thickly muscled thighs and calves revealing themselves as she walked across the gym floor. She wore her regulation coach uniform: athletic shorts like the ones we Vixens wore for practice (though I knew from having helped her place the order that she'd had to source a pair of extra-tall warm-up pants for the encroaching colder weather). Her shirt was a polyester button-down (regulation—it couldn't be helped, even though I'd been lobbying to abolish synthetic materials for *eons* to no avail) in the Bulldog blue and gold. Her dark, curly hair was pinned into an unmoving topknot high on her head. When she reached the bleachers, she scanned the eager-eyed girls and offered a broad wave hello. In response (and in eager curiosity), the Vixens shuffled in their seats, angling to get a good ogle and murmuring confused questions to one another.

I held up my hand, signaling for silence, and the assembled team obliged. "Vixens," I said, smiling, "how better to usher in the new school year than with a new coach?"

A fresh flurry of whispers broke out at that.

"Yes, it's true," I confirmed, ignoring the rising commentary.

I went on, focused. "Coach Grappler comes to us from the warmer climes of sunny Florida, where she single-handedly led no fewer than three separate squads to the top of the national rankings. I just know she's going to do the same for us."

"We're thrilled to welcome you," Principal Honey chimed in.

Now Coach Grappler held her waving hand up, blushing modestly. "I appreciate the glowing introduction, Cheryl—and the welcome, Principal Honey," she said. "But they definitely weren't single-handed victories. I believe in the value of a *team* effort." She placed heavy emphasis on the word *team*, her lips mashing together over the consonants.

"Of course," I agreed. "But surely your own vision was key to the various successes."

She shrugged, seemingly resigned to the flattery, if obviously still not completely comfortable with it.

(I will never understand why some people are so loath to toot their own horns. If we can't be our own biggest champions, pray tell, who will?)

"But, Cheryl," Veronica protested, "this is so . . . out of the blue. A *good* 'out of the blue,'" she added, casting a look at Coach Grappler. "Greetings and salutations, of course, Coach Grappler." She turned back to me. "But exciting as this news is, it's surprising nonetheless. The Vixens have never even *competed* in the nationals before." She glanced around at the rest of the team, looking for either confirmation or contradiction. "Right?"

"Nope," Ginger Lopez said, sleek black ponytail bobbing as she shook her head.

"Don't I know it," I snapped. "And while consistently

placing first in the *regional* division all these years has been a pretty feather in our collective cap, this is *my senior year*. I don't know about you ladies, but *I'm* planning to go out with a bang. Being a big fish in a small pond is all well and good for some of us. But why not aim higher? There's a whole ocean out there, you know."

I watched the emotions flit across her face as Veronica considered the information. I knew, of course, that plenty of my compatriots would just as soon rest on their well-padded laurels senior year rather than go to the effort of gearing up for one final, shining victory lap. But even knowing my spot in my college of choice was secure wasn't enough to deter me or dim my fire. Veronica had La Bonne Nuit and Pop's—other considerations beyond high school. And I would, too, soon enough. But as reigning queen of Riverdale High, I wasn't going to abdicate the throne without adding a few final jewels to my glittering crown.

Betty leaned forward, tentative. "I think it sounds great!" she said, giving a wide smile at Coach Grappler. "I mean, V and I were just saying at breakfast that it's been . . . kind of a rocky road for us in Riverdale these last couple of years. A new coach, some new competitions? That could be totally fun, right? Just normal, regular-high-school-student stuff. We deserve that."

"I couldn't have said it better myself, Betty," I said. "And I love your enthusiasm." I'd lost my dear brother Jay-Jay twice in the last two years: First, literally, when he was brutally murdered at the hands of our own villainous paterfamilias; and then, more symbolically—but no less painfully—when that huckster Svengali Edgar Evernever hypnotized me into thinking Jason was back among the living. (Whether or not I'd fully said my good-byes to him was a different story altogether.) If soaring to the top of a human pyramid in pursuit of a gleaming trophy and a title to match would bring me even a modicum of joy? I was going for it. All the way.

"I hope you'll all join me in making Coach Grappler feel right at home here in Riverdale." I applauded, encouraging the girls to do the same, and the sound of scattered clapping broke out across the room in staggered bursts.

Coach Grappler stepped forward and waved again, still somewhat shy and reserved. "Let me just say, I'm so glad to be here. I've seen videos of your performances, and I'm excited to be working with some real next-level talent. I have a lot of ideas for how to freshen up some of your routines—taking what you're all known for and just turning up the dial with some totally up-to-the-minute choreography and a few more high-powered acrobatic sequences. I know you guys can handle it, and I know it's gonna rock."

Just the mere thought of shiny new dances to practice sent shivers down my spine. It went without saying that the Vixens were known for our halftime dances. With a world-class coach behind us? There was nowhere to go but up. I caught Toni's eye, and she gave me an approving wink.

"Feel free to swing by my office anytime—to ask questions, or even just to say hi."

Principal Honey leaned in at that. "Any time that you're not expected in class, that is."

The girls all gave an obligatory chuckle.

"Absolutely," Coach Grappler echoed, nodding solemnly. "I take cheer *very* seriously, but there's one thing I take more seriously than cheer. And that's your academic performance. I expect excellence from my girls in all areas of their school experience. And I don't believe that extracurricular activities should ever be prioritized over grades."

Even Veronica had to arch an appreciative eyebrow at that—historically, our school could be a wee bit *Friday Night Lights* with its good old boys, giving our football team a little more leeway with non-football-related pursuits than might strictly be considered appropriate. To hear a coach emphasizing the importance of academic excellence was rare enough to be refreshing and quite worthy of respect.

I put my hands on my hips. "And that's not all, ladies. I hope you're all prepared to clear your social calendars for this weekend—*if* they're booked, that is, which I suppose is not necessarily a given."

"What's this weekend?" Veronica asked, still skeptical.

I gave her my most saccharine-sweet grin. "I was just

getting to that, obvi. Coach Grappler has arranged for a special 'Camp Vixens' retreat this weekend at Sweetwater Pines."

Sweetwater Pines was a sleepaway camp about three hours north of Riverdale, nestled deep within the sprawling extended woods of Fox Forest. It tended to attract campers from farther away—people who didn't have as much access to nature as we did on such a regular basis—and as such most Riverdale kids didn't know it well, beyond it being an exit on the interstate one drove past en route to Niagara Falls or similar tourist locales.

Another rush of whispers reverberated across the room as the girls took in this information. No doubt the idea of a cheer retreat was far more exciting and action-packed than whatever sad-John-Hughes-movie plans they'd already made for the weekend, but it *was* short notice, given that today was Friday. That, I could admit.

Betty, in particular, looked gobsmacked. "Cheryl, I mean, that sounds great"—she turned to Coach Grappler, earnest—"and normally, I'd be totally up for it—"

"And what, pray tell, is abnormal about this situation, then?" I cut her off.

She shrugged, a helpless expression on her face. "It's just, I had plans with Jughead. We were hoping to do a Hitchcock double feature."

I shot her my most withering gaze. "*Quelle* yawn. Remind

me why exactly I should care? Isn't that what you and your sad-tramp love interest do *every* weekend? What's the urgency? Surely your fifteenth screening of *Vertigo* will keep."

She shook her head. "It was *The Lady Vanishes* and *North by Northwest*, but that's not the point."

"Then what is?" Tina asked, ever the faithful minion. She'd left her post at the door to Coach Grappler's office to stand at my literal side like the ride-or-die sentinel I'd trained her to be.

"The *point*," Betty went on, "is that with him boarding at Stonewall Prep during the week now, weekends are our only chance to hang out."

I felt a prickle of sympathy. But only a prickle.

"Come on, Cheryl," Veronica chimed in. "I know there's a heart buried *somewhere* inside that ice-princess facade of yours. How would you feel if you and Toni were doing the long-distance love thing? Wouldn't you want to spend every possible moment with her that you could?"

Another small flicker of guilt pulsed in my stomach, but I swallowed it down. Rules were rules, after all—especially rules that *I* created myself. Cheryl Blossom had never deigned to be denied, and she certainly wouldn't start now.

"I'm sympathetic, naturally," I said, hands still on my hips. "But only to a point. Whatever misguided attempts at self-betterment your beau has made that have carried him far from our hallowed Bulldog halls, it's no concern of mine. This weekend is a command performance. Coach Grappler pulled strings to get us access to the camp, and we're not going to let her effort be in vain."

Coach Grappler gave an uncomfortable smile. "Well, it wasn't *too* much effort," she countered. "I know the owners of the camp. It's the off-season, but they're letting us use it for our retreat."

I nodded. "And who are we to turn away this VIP opportunity?" Honestly. Sometimes people could be such hideous ingrates.

Betty shifted in her seat. "But—"

"But nothing." I held up a hand. "Truly, Betty, you should be looking ahead and grateful for the opportunity to have some bonding time with your cohorts. Once your beloved Jughead is gone, the Vixens will be all you have left."

Betty flushed, and Veronica grabbed her hand and gave it a reassuring squeeze.

"Okay," Veronica said, rising. "You can put the dire warnings away. You don't have to prey on Betty's nonexistent relationship insecurities just to get her—to get any of us—to participate in this retreat."

"Good to hear," I quipped. "It's going to be a sheer delight. I promise."

"Cheryl and I have cooked up a lot of fun," Coach Grappler added. "Trust games, cheer drills, campfire stories. All that good stuff."

"I even had a brilliant idea for maple s'mores, as an homage to our hometown heritage." I smiled.

"Um, *yum*," Toni said, grinning. She glanced around the bleachers, drumming up similar smiles from the rest of the group.

"I know." I clasped my hands together tightly and squealed with barely contained glee. "Vixens! I'm just so beyond excited to kick off this school year with a bevy of new Bulldog traditions."

Veronica sighed. "I mean, technically, it's not a 'tradition' if it's new," she said. "That's literally the whole thing about traditions. But your point is well taken, Cheryl. Like I said, I'm in."

"Me too," Betty echoed with a tight smile. "It'll be great. Maple s'mores sound amazing."

Around her, the other Vixens rose to echo the sentiment, smiling and chattering with excitement.

"It *will* be great," I said, beaming broadly. "Just you wait and see."

CHAPTER THREE

JUGHEAD

"I'm sorry—tell me again what *maple s'mores* are? I'll admit, I'm intrigued. Maybe even more than intrigued. Possibly hungry, to be honest. But also slightly confused. Definitely." My stomach grumbled loudly, punctuating the sentiment.

Betty laughed and linked her arm through mine. We were walking from Riverdale High to the town library, a quiet, picturesque stroll down Main Street, to pick up JB and walk her home. When I'd made the plan with her that morning, she insisted she was way too grown up to need her big brother walking her home. But I decided that, in this case, my needs trumped her own—me being the older and arguably wiser big-brother figure in the situation. And I, for one, needed her to have a little bit of normalcy in the absence of anything resembling a stable mom who, you know, hung around and stuff. And anyway, wasn't a big brother being all overprotective and embarrassingly infantilizing sort of peak "normal" for the tween set?

"Yeah, you're not the only confused one. Maple-flavored marshmallows? Syrup on the graham cracker, underneath the chocolate?" Betty shrugged, bringing me back to other urgent concerns, like snacks. "I wish I could tell you, Juggie," she said, "but I think we're just going to have to wait and see."

"Either of those interpretations sounds potentially delicious," I decided. "I'd try it."

She grinned again. "Okay, but is that really saying so much? I mean, I love you, but when it comes to food, you're not exactly known for your discerning tastes."

I smirked. "Fair." I leaned in for a quick kiss. "Thank goodness the same can't be said for my choice in romantic partners."

"Thank goodness," she agreed, laughing again. "There's something we can both agree on. *And* you're such a charmer." She snuggled in closer, so I could smell the deep floral tones of her shampoo and the vanilla-laced bite of her perfume. "It's just . . . you *just* got home from Stonewall. I wish I didn't have to turn around and leave town the morning after you get here."

"You and me both." *Why* had I left all this—*her*—behind for Stonewall Prep, again? Was I genuinely insane? Sometimes it felt that way.

A world-class education, I reminded myself, trying in vain not to breathe in the nearness of Betty as we walked. *The chance to be the first Jones ever to go to college. An opportunity for something bigger, something better.*

I wasn't leaving Betty behind, not in the long run. That was

41

what I had to keep telling myself. Taking a once-in-a-lifetime chance to succeed in ways I previously hadn't allowed myself to dream? Well, that would only make me *more* worthy of someone as amazing, unique, and insanely smart as Betty, wouldn't it? It would be a good thing for both of us. Eventually, that is—in some sort of vague, ephemeral future that I *had* to keep reminding myself still lay in wait for the two of us. It would be great. It would make us stronger.

Wouldn't it?

"Where'd you go, Jug?" Betty burst into my thoughts with another kiss of her own, which I eagerly reciprocated. "I lost you there for a minute. If this is the only time we get together this weekend, we can't afford to waste it."

"I'm here," I promised, giving her arm an extra squeeze. "Just . . . sad we're not going to get to have our Netflix-and-chill tomorrow like we planned."

"Me too," she admitted. "But I think the retreat is a good idea, even if it weren't for this new coach. Some bonding time for the Vixens."

"Yeah."

"I mean, we keep saying we want to get back to 'normal,' just do, you know . . . dumb high school stuff . . . That's what this retreat is, after all."

"The same could be said about a good binge-watch with your significant other," I pointed out, "but I totally hear you. I support this decision, and I can't wait to hear all about it.

Ooh—" I started, a thought occurring to me. "Do you think you'll do trust falls?" The idea of it made me briefly yearn for a Kafkaesque metamorphosis into a fly on the proverbial cabin wall.

"That would require Cheryl to have a drop of trust in any of her fellow squad members," Betty said. "Which . . . seems unlikely. But I will be sure to let you know. *And* I promise to take notes on the recipe for maple s'mores, and any other interesting snacks that come up."

"That's my girl." My stomach growled again, and we both laughed.

"So, what do you think you'll do tomorrow night while I'm away?" Betty asked.

"Other than lock myself in my room and listen to angsty eighties new-wave sorrow-pop, staring at your picture?" I teased. "Just get my brood on?"

"Obviously. *Other* than broody angst."

"No idea. I mean, you just dropped this on me, so I haven't had a chance to come up with a plan B. I'll call Archie, see what he's up to."

"Good idea," Betty said. "Veronica's worried about him. I am, too, if I'm being honest. He's still grieving, even though he tries not to show it."

"That doesn't surprise me," I replied. "That he's having a hard time and putting on a brave face for us."

"So maybe some male-bonding time will be good for you,"

Betty said. "Even if he doesn't want to talk about it, just, you know, being with you. It might help." She kissed me. "It always helps *me*."

"I'll see what he's up to, figure something out," I promised. "I should maybe make some time to write, too. Read, for sure. Catch up on homework—this prep school thing is no joke. And, I don't know—check in with Sweet Pea. See what's new with the gang. That is, if there's any time left before I have to head back to Stonewall on Sunday."

"Ah." She paused. "How are things with the Serpents?" she asked, careful.

"You mean, how's our low-key civil war with the Pretty Poisons progressing? Despite our temporary cease-fire when we came together to defeat the Gargoyle King on prom night?"

"Well, yeah," she admitted. "But I think you just answered my question," she said, rueful.

As Betty knew, Toni Topaz and I had temporarily aligned our respective gangs at the end of last year so that the Pretty Poisons and the Southside Serpents could work together toward common goals rather than waste precious time—and valuable resources—with petty infighting. The Gargoyle King was gone now—but continued collaboration and cooperation were still a work in progress. It turned out everyone wanted their own gang to be number one. It was hard to make that math work all the time.

"We're, uh, getting there," I said, trying for optimism.

"That bad, huh?" Betty made a sympathetic noise.

"It's *not* that bad, honestly," I said. "Everyone's intentions are good. Mostly. It's just . . . people are used to what they're used to. And some of what they're used to is, you know, power."

"No one wants to give it up," Betty surmised.

"Can you blame them? When is anyone ever looking to relinquish control, especially when it means buddying up with your rivals? Exhibit A: the whole, entire history of mankind. It's just one long, bloody, endless power grab."

Betty shrugged. "Touché. But I don't know . . ." Her pace slowed as she considered her words. "Sometimes I feel like I spend so much of my life trying to keep every little flicker of emotion under control. If you told me I could just let go? I don't know if I'd fight it."

Now I slowed to a full stop and turned her so we were face-to-face. I put my hands on her shoulders. I brushed a strand of hair that had wriggled free from her ponytail back off her forehead. She gazed at me, her eyes piercing right into my core.

"Betty Cooper," I said, my voice low, "you know that if you ever need to let go, I'm here for you."

"I know, Juggie," she said. "And that's why I love you."

We stayed like that for a few beats, forehead to forehead, breathing the same fall air. Neither of us wanted to move, to break the spell, I knew. But the buzz of my phone in my back pocket shook me and reminded me that there was actually a reason we'd come to the library in the first place.

I held up my phone so Betty could see it. "I think my dad's been spending too much time with JB. His texts have devolved into tweenspeak." I showed her the screen, a note about JB running late followed by the namaste-hands emoji and a winking emoji.

Betty laughed. "I'll be worried when it's you and the emojis are cat faces. This? This is cute."

"Who's cute?"

We looked up to see JB walking toward us, a mischievous glint in her eyes as she shoved her phone deep in her pocket. "You're late," I called reflexively.

Betty gave me a look of reproach and drove an elbow into my rib.

"Just chill, Jug," she said, sotto voce.

"I'm like ten minutes late. Dad was supposed to tell you. Relax." JB was utterly unperturbed by my low-key reprimand.

"And"—I turned and pointed at the doorway of the library— "you're not coming from the library, which was where we agreed to meet. Change of plans?" I tried to keep my voice light, but I wasn't fooling anyone.

JB rolled her eyes. "Whatever. I was with Ricky."

"Ricky DeSantos?" I said, realizing. "The one who introduced you to Gryphons and Gargoyles?"

"The one who helped you *defeat the Gargoyle King*, in the end," she countered. "Remember?"

It was true enough. But it wasn't the whole story. "Fair. But also—the one who stabbed Archie, *right*?"

She flushed. "Look, he's sorry about that. You know he had to. Or, he thought he did, at the time. And I think he's totally proven himself since then."

"And I'm sure Archie's forgiven him for that," Betty said, stepping in smoothly. She gave me another meaningful look as she put a hand on JB's shoulder. "Which means we should, too. *Right,* Jug?"

"Right," I said, with only slightly less enthusiasm than Betty had managed to muster.

Betty went on. "I know Jughead is *totally fine* with you meeting up with your friends after school. I mean, that's a *normal, healthy* thing to do. He just . . . worries, you know."

JB sighed. "Great. Well, can you please remind my brother that we're not, like, living in ye olden days? I mean, he can look out for me without, like, totally stalking me twenty-four hours of the day. Right?"

"I can definitely remind him," Betty agreed, "though I'm pretty sure he just got the message loud and clear."

"He did," I chimed in. "And he's also not super into talking about himself in the third person."

JB rolled her eyes at me. "I'm talking to you directly

now: Jug, I'm basically a Serpent. You *don't* need to be so obsessed with watching out for me. I can handle myself."

I held up a hand. "Don't get ahead of yourself," I said. "If anything, you're a Serpent-in-Training."

Betty stepped forward, jumping in to smooth the conversation over. "Why argue semantics?" she said, looking back and forth between the two of us. "How about instead, we all just agree that the next time JB's plans change, she'll send you a text directly rather than letting you hear about it from FP?"

"A perfectly reasonable proposition," I agreed. "I won't give you a hard time—well, probably not, anyway," I amended quickly. "But I do want to be kept in the loop."

She narrowed her eyes at me. "Control freak."

I gave her a playful shove. "I prefer to think of it as brotherly love."

Control. Power. It's what everyone wants. The lust to be the alpha, to dominate, to be the one who controls the reins? It's a seductive notion. Epic. The stuff of legends.

The stuff of this legend, to be precise.

Or, if you prefer, it's like a fairy tale. Any fairy tale; strip them down and they're all the same at their fractured, beating cores. They begin with "Once upon a time." They unfold in the woods outside a rich kingdom, one filled with an interchangeable cast of characters: fair maidens striving to impress; a princess supreme, unassailable and sublime; and a beast, ignored until it's too late.

These fairy tales are full of petty jealousies, rivalries, and frayed loyalties. Passions are pushed to the breaking point—boiling over, erupting like a broken promise or a violent, divine-sent storm. Deadly games. A victim's disregarded plea. An infernal baptism.

And the finale: consequences, deep and indelible as a road map of scarred skin.

This particular fairy tale is about a poor peasant girl, not of noble birth. She was a misfit, posturing amid the royal court.

The ladies-in-waiting weren't charmed; they weren't willing to accept an outsider into their ranks. A peasant could never be more than a scullery maid. To suggest as much was laughable at best.

At worst, it was treasonous.

They toyed with her, playing collective cat to her mouse. They dangled promises before her—just enough to secure her loyalty. Just enough to ensure she'd never go to the elders and speak of the things they did to her.

And, oh, the things they did to her.

It wasn't enough that she should be subdued, you see. For their purposes, for their own sordid sense of security, for them to remain fully in power . . .

For that she needed to be silenced, eternally.

Once upon a time . . . *You've heard the story. I promise, you know this.*

Soon you'll know me, too.

CHAPTER FOUR

Jughead:

Hey, Arch—when the girls are away, the guys'll . . . I don't know, bro-out in some random, excessively gendered form of male bonding?

Archie:

Sounds fun, Jug—I think? But I'm still hauling ass trying to keep on top of the community center and stuff. Rain check?

Jughead:

Archie! This is a unique opportunity. I'm home from Stonewall AND the girls are away. Who knows when we'll have a chance like this again?

Archie:

True. OK. I get what you're saying.

Jughead:

Great, so . . . ideas? Of the two of us, you're definitely the bro-ier one.

Archie:

OK, man. I'll take that as a compliment.
How about . . . I don't know, poker?
We can invite Reggie, Sweet Pea, Munroe,
maybe Kevin . . . make it a thing.

Jughead:

That does sound perfectly masculine. And I'm
all for opening the invitation up, especially in
the interests of a solid poker game. But let's
not make the game TOO big, yeah? You
know I'm not exactly a social butterfly.

Archie:

Trust me: I know, man. We'll put together
a boys night to make you proud.

Jughead:

Side note: Let's definitely not call it a boys night.

Archie:

Dude, you read my mind.

ᴧᴧᴧ

ARCHIE

As soon as I'd hit "send" on my last text to Jughead, I had headed over to Veronica's. I was sitting in her desk chair turned toward her bed, watching her pack for the Vixens retreat. She was leaving early tomorrow morning, and I was bummed to miss her for the weekend. Even if Jughead and I now had guy plans straight out of a Judd Apatow movie.

"Ronnie, you think you've got enough sweaters there?" I teased.

She patted the topmost sweater on the pile—it was literally the fifth she'd stacked in her suitcase, now so thick I was starting to wonder how she was going to get the thing closed—and looked at me. Her eyes were wide and bright behind her tortoiseshell glasses.

"Better safe than sorry, Archiekins," she chirped. "There are few things worse than being caught in the wilds, unawares—or, at least, so I'd imagine. And speaking from *extensive* personal experience, there are also, most *definitely*, much worse crosses to bear than finding oneself with a surplus of Mongolian cashmere on hand." Her eyes twinkled. I watched as she wrangled the top of the suitcase down and zipped it effortlessly. Obviously I'd underestimated her packing skills.

"I guess there's no harm in being overprepared," I agreed. "But, I mean, it's camp, Veronica. Sleepaway camp. It's not *Into the Wild*."

"From your beautiful lips to God's and Gabbana's ears," she quipped. "But have you been listening to the weather report? It's slowly but surely going from mildly dismal to absolutely dire. That storm they were predicting isn't getting any smaller. Just the opposite, actually; RIVW was saying something about upgrading it from 'severe weather' to 'high winds and flood threats.'"

"I know, I heard. But don't worry, you'll be in bunks. And the weather guys always exaggerate that stuff, anyway."

I tried to sound reassuring. I could tell that underneath her New York–sophisticate bravado she was actually a little nervous. "You're right, though—the more sweaters the merrier. Clearly I'm nuts. Go big or go home."

"That's basically the philosophy I'm going with, in a nutshell."

"I'm convinced," I agreed.

"So," I said, moving from the desk to the bed. I settled myself at the head, leaning back against her tufted headboard, careful not to knock any piles of clothing over. "Other than the weather—and missing me—are you looking forward to getting away at all?"

She pursed her lips, thinking. "Honestly? Yes." She grinned. "I'm as surprised as anyone. And not just because I'm basically the least likely candidate to go for a wilderness retreat ever. The Wakaya ecolodge in Fiji is pretty much as close to nature as this girl gets." She closed her eyes, no doubt remembering some luxurious vacation highlights of the past. "We have to go there sometime, Archie," she said. "Maybe as a graduation present." She wiggled her eyebrows. "Catch of the day for dinner every night."

"I love fishing," I said. Her enthusiasm was totally infectious, as usual. Even though fishing reminded me of catch-and-release afternoons along the banks of Sweetwater River with my dad . . .

I shook my head. I was supposed to be reassuring Veronica right now, not going off into some pity party inside my own mind. "But until we can get to Wakaya—I've got poker night, and you've got the world's largest collection of sweaters."

"Yep. It should be fun. Cheryl is definitely going to be her usual high-drama self, but B and I are due for some quality female bonding. A road trip with the Vixens, a weekend in a normal little high school bubble? I think this retreat will hit the spot." She paused, her mood seeming to fall slightly. "But of course, I'll miss having my usual cuddle time with you." She rubbed my arm. "I hate leaving you alone."

"I'll be okay," I insisted, even though down deep, I wasn't sure. "Especially if Jughead has anything to say about it."

"And apparently, he does," Veronica agreed. She picked her suitcase up and placed it neatly by the bedroom doorway. I guessed Smithers would probably pack it in the car for her.

Veronica came back around to where I was sitting on the

bed, putting her hands on my shoulders. A little shiver went through me when she touched me; that feeling never got old.

She reached a soft hand under my chin and tilted my face up, looking me dead in the eyes. Her hair fell in dark waves over her shoulders, and her expression was tender but concerned. I knew that expression very well.

"I can't begin to imagine what you're going through, Archiekins," she began. She spoke slowly, carefully, like she knew it was a loaded topic and she wanted to tread lightly. "I know you want to keep busy. And I know how important it is to you to have the community center up and running smoothly."

"Not just running," I corrected her. *"Thriving."*

"It's a noble endeavor," she said, running her hands through my hair.

"Sure." I glanced away. Maybe it was: making a space for kids to gather, kids who had nowhere else to go, no good options, and no safe spaces? Yeah, that was a worthy goal. But the truth was, I had my own selfish reasons for throwing myself into the community center these days, too.

Because other than Ronnie, the community center was kind of all I had left. And I had to put my energy somewhere, didn't I? Some place other than staring into space all night, listening to my clock tick, thinking about my dad? Missing him? Turning it around and around in my head—the idea that I was never going to see him again.

I blinked. The last thing I needed was for Ronnie to see me tear up. She was worried enough about me as it was.

"It *is*," she insisted, turning my head back toward her so she could look in my eyes. "But, Archiekins—you're burning the candle at both ends. Especially the way you've been overseeing the Andrews Construction stuff, too."

I swallowed. Of course, I was overseeing the construction stuff. Who else would, now?

"There's barely any wick left, to beat a metaphor to death. And the thing is—I spoke to your mom."

"You did?" This was news to me. Obviously the two of them spent time together when Veronica was at my house and stuff, and my mom loved her. But the idea that they were having heart-to-heart conversations when I wasn't around? Yeah, it felt a little weird.

"I assure you, I wasn't going behind your back or anything like that," Veronica insisted, "but I do see her. I'm your girl-friend, after all."

"That much, I actually know." I grinned.

"Well, so, we're in contact. Not in any premeditated way, but it happens. For instance, like last week, that night we all ordered a pizza? And you were out walking Vegas while we waited for the food?"

I remembered. "Yeah, I remember. And you and my mom—you guys were inside setting the table."

She nodded. "Exactly. Anyway . . . we talked. We *do* talk.

And she was saying that the business is doing fine. Your commitment has already paid off tenfold. And the community center *is* thriving, just like you envisioned, just like you wanted. All your hard work . . . it's *worked*. Everything is in great shape."

And she was right—everything *was* in good shape. Unless, you know, you counted . . . well, *me*.

But I couldn't admit that to Veronica; I couldn't admit that to anyone. I couldn't bear for them to be any more worried than they already were.

"So"—she tilted her head to deliver the caveat that was so clearly on its way—"you *don't* need to keep up this . . . I don't know, this constant self-flagellation. Will you please take this one weekend off to have some fun with your friends?"

My heart flooded, hearing her talk. I hated that she was worried about me, but it was still comforting, how much she cared.

"You're very persuasive." I kissed her on the forehead. "So, yes, I will try to enjoy my poker night with the guys. Jughead actually agreed to open it up a bit, invite some of the Serpents, Reggie. You know, small but fun."

"I like it!" Her eyes flashed. "Just one thought. Or rather," she clarified, "more of a question, actually: Where are you guys going to play? Did you have a location in mind?"

I shrugged. "I don't know. We basically *just* decided on it.

The community center, I guess? I mean, that would be fine. It's just a few of us, you know?"

She frowned. "Right. And *fine* is . . . well, fine, I suppose. But maybe we can do better than that."

"Better than *fine*?"

"Come on—where's your sense of occasion?"

"I . . . don't have one?" I said. *Or if I did, I guess I'd lost it . . . right around the time I lost my dad.*

"What are you getting at?" I asked. I was definitely getting the feeling our low-key poker night was about to be kicked up to the next level.

She shrugged. "The girls are going to be off on our wilderness adventure, why not turn your ad hoc poker night into a full-on . . . well, a real, full-on Poker Night? You can keep your guest list small—if you *must*. But we can still take it to the next level. Why not?"

Next level. Did I know my girl, or what? I thought about it. Maybe she *did* have a point . . . ? "What did you have in mind?"

"Have it at La Bonne Nuit!"

"The speakeasy?"

"Of course! It's perfect. Make it a whole event! Themed cocktails, a dress code, passed canapés, the works."

"Good luck talking Jughead into respecting a *dress code*. And if you think either of us knows how to make canapés, sorry, but you're in for a rude awakening."

"Okay, forget the dress code. But Pop can arrange the food. You won't have to lift a finger."

"Okay," I said, relenting. "We'll have it at the speakeasy. We'll have Pop-approved snacks. But nothing, you know, too *crazy*. Otherwise it'll be the last guys night Jughead ever agrees to."

She rolled her eyes. "Not to be reductionist, but I think it's safe to say that once he hears about the canapés, he'll be all in."

"Good point."

We were both laughing when we heard a soft rapping at the bedroom door.

"Come in," Veronica called. To me she turned and said, by way of explanation, "Smithers."

The door swung open and—yep—Smithers walked in, an enormous feast from Pop's spread across a large silver platter in his arms. The smell was indescribable—chargrilled beef and gooey cheese and a hint of chocolate syrup from one of the milk shakes sweating beads of condensation down their sides. My stomach growled automatically. I hadn't even realized I was starving, but now that I thought about it, it dawned on me that I'd skipped breakfast to make those early-morning construction deliveries. And I'd barely had a minute to scarf down a sandwich at lunch, since I was busy catching up on homework. No wonder the sight of those burgers was making me drool.

"Amazing timing, Smithers," I said, clearing space on Veronica's desk to take the tray from him. "How did you know?"

"Miss Veronica had asked me to bring an early supper in for the two of you while she packed," Smithers explained. "I believe she said it 'very well might be the last decent bite of food she had all weekend.'"

"Not hyperbolic at all." Veronica laughed and snatched an onion ring from the tray, steam rising up from it in curls. "What can I say? I'll no doubt be dreaming of this meal this time tomorrow night, when we're relegated to . . ." She faltered. "Actually? I confess: I don't even know what they serve at camp."

"You'll probably roast hot dogs over a campfire at some point," I told her. "It's classic. So, maybe not *that* different from Pop's." I pointed to the two chili dogs on the tray, smothered in relish.

"Okay, so maybe I won't starve to death," she conceded. "But I'm willing to bet this Pop's chili dog is better than any I'll roast at Sweetwater Pines."

"No argument here," I said. "I'll save my betting for poker night."

"Wise," Veronica said. "And also, an excellent segue. Smithers, Archie and his friends are going to have a gathering at La Bonne Nuit tomorrow night. A boys poker night, as he says. Do you think you'd be able to coordinate some of the particulars with Pop for him while I'm away? Mostly the food and beverage orders, and confirming details about the security system. It should be simple, really. Reggie's going to be there, right?" She looked at me.

"Right. But . . . security system?" I asked, puzzled. "It's a poker night with my high school buddies, not a Danny Ocean movie."

"Just standard operating procedure, Archiekins. What can I say? I'm my father's daughter, no matter how much I may resist that fact from time to time. I invested in a state-of-the-art system for the whole building when I bought the deed to Pop's and opened La Bonne Nuit. Reggie's very familiar with it; he can get you up to speed."

"Right, cool," I said. I was doing my best to sound indifferent, but the truth was, thinking about Reggie being Veronica's right hand at the speakeasy? It wasn't the best feeling. Too much of a reminder of how they'd been together for a little while . . . and how, if Reggie'd had his way, they still would be.

If Veronica sensed any shift in my mood, though, she didn't let on. "So, Smithers, what do you think? Would you be able to help with that?"

"Of course. I would be glad to, Miss Veronica," Smithers said. He turned to address me directly. "Please don't worry about a thing, Master Andrews."

"I won't, Smithers."

"Excellent. Now"—he reached into the lapel pocket of his uniform jacket—"in the meantime, though, I did also want to deliver this letter to you, Miss Veronica."

He fished a nondescript white envelope from his pocket and held it out to her. "It came today while you were at school. And it seemed to me to be something you'd want to see . . . *before* you left for the weekend."

Something about the tone in his voice sounded loaded, meaningful. I could tell Veronica was thinking the same thing. Her eyes narrowed as she took the letter from him. She turned the envelope over in her hand, studying the return address. "Shankshaw Prison." She sighed. "Well, that can only mean one person. The person I'm *least* interested in hearing from."

"Speak of the devil," I said.

Hiram Lodge was in maximum security—where we all hoped he'd rot, indefinitely, even if we tried our best not to say as much to Ronnie. The letter had to be from him. And there was no way it was good news. Nothing that came from Hiram Lodge ever was.

She held the letter out in front of her for a minute, considering it. Then she sighed heavily and ripped the flap open, pulling the letter out.

The room was quiet while her eyes darted back and forth across the sheet of paper, scanning. By the time she'd finished reading the letter, her mouth was set in a grim line. Slowly, without saying a single word, she crumpled the paper into a ball in her fist. She tossed the crumpled ball into the wastebasket under her desk almost without effort, hardly glancing as it ricocheted against the sides of the can and slid down. She shook her head, frustrated.

"Do you . . . want to talk about it?" I asked. Truthfully, even though I knew, deep down, it wasn't my fault—and Ronnie had insisted as much, a million times—I still sometimes felt guilty for how far apart he and Veronica were these days.

"Frankly, I don't even know what to say," she said. She shook her head, weary. "Just when I think he couldn't possibly stoop any lower or find any other way to get under my skin. Somehow, there's always a new twist. It's classic Hiram Lodge, basically—a seemingly innocent missive to his beloved daughter, *'just checking in,* m'hija,' and inquiring as to her well-being."

"*Seemingly*," I repeated.

"Sure," Veronica went on. "To the casual observer, the letter seems pleasant . . . maybe even loving. But I know my father. I'm all-too-well-versed in his personal brand of subtext. Asking how I'm doing? Telling me he 'hopes I'm well on-course for a fruitful, exciting senior year'?"

"Fruitful?"

She smirked. "I'm not a fool. This little love note is Daddy's way of telling me not to get too comfortable in his absence. She looked at me. "Which, believe me, was *not* on the menu."

"And speaking of menu," Smithers said, cutting into the conversation in an obvious attempt to smooth over some of the tension in the air, "why don't I just go call Pop now and get started on that poker night selection?"

"Thanks, Smithers, you're a lifesaver," Veronica said, grateful.

"Yeah—thank you," I added as he moved to the door. "But, seriously—it's just me and Jughead and a few of the guys. Like, it definitely doesn't have to be a big thing."

"Absolutely not, Master Andrews. Understood. I'll take care of all the details. Just leave it to me."

As he closed the door behind him, Veronica gave me a wink. I know "not a big thing" in Lodge-verse was way different from what it meant to me. But my poker night had somehow turned into Veronica's gift to me. I was in her hands now, metaphorically speaking. It was best to sit back, let go, and enjoy the ride.

~~~

Reggie:

Bro, Veronica tells me poker night's been moved to La Bonne Nuit and you need me to run you through the security system?

Archie:

Uh, yeah. She says you know how it all works.

Reggie:

Don't worry, I can show you the ropes.
I can definitely also mix a few of my
signature drinks, too—if you ask nicely.

Archie:

I mean, if you want to, that's great.
I'm sure we can handle drinks and
stuff, though, if it's too much for you.

Reggie:

That's hilarious. I AM too much, man.
You know that.

Archie:

I hope you're not waiting for me to argue with you.

Reggie:

Reggie Mantle waits for no man. Anyway,
see you there. (Unless you want to just
straight give me all your money now?)

Archie:

Yeah, yeah. Hilarious. Let's just wait and see.
We'll find out who the big winner is.

〜〜〜

Reggie:

Yo, Bulldogs, you heard it here first: poker night at La Bonne Nuit TONIGHT. Come early so I can take all your money.

〜〜〜

Chuck:

Yo, Arch, what's the buy-in for the game tonight?

Chuck:

Reggie was saying something like $20? That feels a little rich for my blood.

Archie:

When did you talk to Reggie about the poker game?

Chuck:

He sent out a group text to the whole team to let us know about it.

Archie:

Of course he did . . .

〜〜〜

Jug—just a little warning. You might have already heard, but our small poker night appears to be getting bigger by the second. Once we moved it to La Bonne Nuit for a more, uh, "festive" touch, the guest list kind of spiraled. Chuck just told me Reggie passed the invite on to all the Bulldogs.

Jughead:

That's not all—I just got a text from Peaches 'N Cream. She heard from Sweet Pea that the Serpents were coming tonight and wanted to know why the Pretty Poisons were left off the list. So TLDR: They're coming, too.

Archie:

Like Veronica says, the more the merrier?

Jughead:

Yeah, because Veronica and I have always had such similar attitudes toward social outings.

Archie:

What do you want me to do, man? It's a little too late to call it off, I think.

Jughead:

It's DEFINITELY too late, if only because I'm pretty sure Kevin Keller invited some RROTC kid he made friends with over the summer and he'd murder us if his big date night vanished.

Jughead:

So don't do that.

Archie:

You're OK with a whole big thing?

Jughead:

What the hell? Even this social recluse can hang once in a while.

Archie:

Cool. It'll be fun, I promise.

Jughead:

I love your vision, Arch. May your confidence be manifested into glorious reality. Until tomorrow . . .

∿∿∿

Betty:

So, you got the invite to the poker game? Archie told me you're bringing a DATE?

Kevin:

Archie has a big mouth.

Betty:

Not a date, then?

Kevin:

I mean, not NOT a date. It's Frankie Valdez. He was in RROTC with Moose and me.

Betty:

How did you get from RROTC pal to poker night plus-one?

Kevin:

OMG, you're SUCH a gossip queen!

Kevin:

Luckily for you, so am I.

Kevin:

If you MUST know, I found his profile on GrindEm.

Betty:

All the way to the internet just to meet another Riverdale High student . . .

Kevin:

Tell me about it.

Kevin:

At least you can't complain about this one.
He's a known quantity. Well, relatively known.

Betty:

No complaints. I'm just glad you're going out.

Kevin:

Way to make me sound like a charity case, Betts.
😔 I want it on the record that I'm feeling a touch
excessively parented by you.

Betty:

After everything we've been through, especially
recently, can you blame me? I'm just looking
out for you. But your point is taken and I'll try
to back off a little.

Kevin:

I'm holding you to that.

Betty:

Text me updates. Not sure about service in
the woods, but I want details if I can get
them!

Kevin:

You DEFINITELY won't get service, but I'll DEFINITELY try. Will need someone to vent to if things get crazy! And, I mean . . . this is Riverdale so . . .

Betty:

Yeah, "crazy" is kind of our town motto. Fingers crossed for you.

Kevin:

Ditto! Don't wash away—they're saying the storm is going to be EPIC.

Betty:

Just my luck. Off to pack some serious waterproof gear.

CHAPTER FIVE

Jughead:

All the Serpents are in for poker night. And Poisons, too, now. I'm a little worried about the tension. Even a friendly card game can get a little intense, you know?

Betty:

Well, maybe this will be a chance to smooth over some of the ruffled feathers?

Jughead:

We'll see. Munroe is coming, too, and a bunch of Archie's boxing buddies . . . not to mention Kevin and his mystery date. AND some of the theater crew AND Reggie and the Bulldogs. Honestly, at this point, I don't even know half the people on the guest list.

Betty:

I guess that's what they call a "full house."

Jughead:

groan

Jughead:

Excellent dad joke, Betty. Sincerely.

Betty:

Anytime. ☺

Jughead:

Seriously, though, it'll (probably) be fun to hang with Archie—and, you know, basically half the town's teen population, from the sound of it—but I'm still bummed not to have the weekend with you.

Betty:

Don't remind me. Same, obviously. But it's OK. We're going to be fine. You know what they say, distance makes the heart grow fonder.

Betty:

And I'll be EXTRA fond of you after a weekend of cheer camp and Cheryl in full Head Bombshell mode. I can basically assure you of that.

Jughead:

When it comes to the Vixens, it's definitely Cheryl's world, we're just living in it.

∿∿∿

Sweet Pea:

Everyone's in for poker night. And, man—I know we're, like, supposed to all be totally over the whole us vs. them thing with the Northsiders—but I gotta say, our boys are looking forward to taking those Bulldogs' cash.

Jughead:

I'd be lying if I said that wasn't understandable. But let's keep all nice and friendly, OK?

Sweet Pea:

Got it. And I'll make sure the rest of the gang knows.

Sweet Pea:

But speaking of nice and friendly . . .

Jughead:

Well, that's an auspicious segue. What now?

Sweet Pea:

It's just . . . things are a little tense with the Pretty Poisons. STILL a little tense, I mean . . . Those girls did come for us, remember?

Jughead:

Come on, man—we made a truce. The Pretty Poisons and the Serpents are on the same team from here on out. Can't you guys just respect that?

Sweet Pea:

I'm not saying we couldn't try harder—and I can talk to the gang about that, too—but you could also talk to the Poisons, is all I'm saying. It takes two. Or, uh, it takes two SIDES, anyway. And aren't you our King? Meaning, this is kinda on you to handle, anyway?

Jughead:

Sweet Pea, you're killing me here. You know now that I'm at Stonewall, I'm spread pretty thin. I'm always here for the Serpents, but I don't have time for petty babysitting. You guys have to get it together and learn how to handle things on your own.

Sweet Pea:

Yeah, OK, we will. Geez, you don't have to be so dramatic about it. It's just something that's going on. I thought you'd want to know about it. Isn't that what you said? Keep you looped in and everything?

Jughead:

I know what I said, but this is ridiculous. I just want to know when it's under control, OK?

Sweet Pea:

Sure, OK. Will do.

Jughead:

See you tomorrow night at the game.

Sweet Pea:

Yup.

∼∼∼

BETTY

I try not to be too superstitious. There's enough *real*, tangible bad stuff out there in the world without getting all worked up imagining that we're seeing signs in secret places or that we've been, I don't know, marked by fate somehow. But the bus trip to Sweetwater Pines didn't get off to a particularly promising start, and it was hard *not* to read too much into that.

It was Saturday morning, and everyone was gathered in the Riverdale High parking lot to wait for our bus to take us to the retreat. But when Veronica arrived at the pickup, she was already looking pretty shaken up. It was easy enough to distract ourselves loading luggage once the bus had arrived—our own, and helping the rest of the Vixens, who were looking a little panicked at the rain that had already begun to fall in relentless sheets. The weather reports weren't getting any more optimistic, and if this was just the start of it . . . well, it looked like we might be in for more nature this weekend than we'd bargained for. Everyone's hair was already clinging to their scalps in scraggly wet tangles, and more than a few people's once-perfect mascara had begun to trail sooty tracks down their cheeks.

Between the rain and the loading of the luggage (it must be said: As a group, the Vixens do *not* pack light), V and I couldn't really talk about what was bothering her. Luckily, we had a three-hour drive ahead of us, which gave us plenty of time to catch up on all issues, large and small alike.

Trying in vain to shake the excess water off our umbrellas, we filed as quickly as we could onto the bus. Coach Grappler had planted herself in the driver's seat (she was as hands-on and DIY as it got, it was turning out), waving us down the aisle in a manner that managed to somehow be both welcoming and still slightly intimidating, all at the same time. While everyone else looked like—at best—drowned rats, somehow Coach's topknot looked perfectly sleek and deliberate, rather than athletic and utilitarian, which I suspected was her actual intention. Her warm-up suit was crisp and already nearly dry, tiny residual beads of water sluicing down her sleeves almost gracefully.

(Meanwhile, my own windbreaker was stuck to my torso like a soggy second skin.)

"It's gonna be a great weekend, girls," she said, giving me a warm smile that felt almost specifically directed as I passed by. I tried to match her grin, even though my socks were squelching in my sneakers with every step and I wasn't exactly feeling my smiley-est. I mean, she'd *just* started this new job and, right away, to dive headfirst into a road trip slash cheer camp retreat with a bunch of girls she barely knew? By choice? That was brave. She deserved at least a grin for that effort.

"Thanks, Coach," I said. "V—how about here?" I indicated two seats up at the front of the bus, knowing Veronica tended to get carsick toward the back.

"Perfect, B—" she started, passing me her small duffel to put on her designated seat. But she was quickly cut off by Her Highness herself—HBIC Cheryl.

"Out of our way, underlings!" Cheryl shouted, imperious. Somehow, she, too, managed to look less like the hot mess that the rest of us were and more like a tragic heroine of a gothic novel. Her signature scarlet lipstick was still impeccable, and even wet, her red waves tumbled down her shoulders with the drama of a silent-film femme fatale. *It figures*, I thought, curling my toes in my sneakers and feeling the water surge between them.

"What's your damage, Heather?" Veronica quipped, joking, but only partly. She rolled her eyes at Cheryl's typical histrionics.

"Shoo, little flies," she said to us, waving her hand to underscore her point. "Everyone knows that the front-most seats on a Vixens road trip are reserved for *moi* . . . and a plus-one of my own designation. In this case, clearly *mon petit trésor*, Antoinette."

Over Cheryl's shoulder, Toni flashed us a sympathetic look, mouthing, *Sorry*. She put a hand on Cheryl's back. "Babe, I mean, thanks—I love that you've got my back and all. But, maybe bring it down to an eight? I think they get the point. No one needs to come to blows over a seat on a school bus."

"Indeed. We get it." Veronica gave a tight smile. "Loud and clear, Cheryl," she said. She gestured for me to pass her duffel back to her and for us to shift down a few rows, out of range of Cheryl's warpath but still in the safety zone for Veronica's delicate constitution.

It was only a few more minutes—and, seemingly unavoidably, a few more ruffled feathers here and there (but just a few, thank goodness)—and then, at last, we were officially on our way. With a cough of exhaust that punctuated a momentary break in the roiling thunder outside, we pulled out of the parking lot and onto Main Street, barreling toward the turnpike as fast as the ominous weather would permit.

∿∿∿

"So you really think your father was trying to mess with your head, sending you that letter?"

We'd been driving down the highway for maybe an hour or so, but the storm showed no signs of letting up. Lightning forked the horizon in the distance, and the bus was inching along slowly, less of a cruise and more of a crawl. We'd passed Greendale a ways back, prompting a shudder of déjà vu to slide down my spine as the road sign registered in my peripheral vision. Weird things always seemed to happen in and around the place—weird even by Riverdale standards, which was saying something.

But I couldn't be distracted by that just now. Shaking off that lurking sense of dread that had draped itself over my shoulders as best I could, I turned back to V and forced myself to focus. "What did it say?"

She shrugged. "Honestly, the content was benign enough. *How are you? I miss you,* et cetera . . . the usual, pretending to be a loving patriarch." Her voice dripped with scorn. "You know my father. He's a master at keeping up appearances and subtle innuendo . . . *Nothing to see here.*"

"But . . . he misses you. I'm sure that on some level he means that," I tried to reassure her.

She pursed her lips. "Right, I mean, he's basically the devil incarnate . . . but deep down, he *does* love me, is that it?" She shrugged. "I guess that's some cold comfort, anyway."

"You know he does. He has to." It was what I told myself, after all. What I *had* to tell myself, given everything I'd gone through with my own father.

Still. I had my doubts. So I didn't blame Veronica for having her own.

Case in point. She turned to me, her eyes intent. "I'd love to think so, B. But I'm not sure it's true. It's just . . . how many unforgivable acts does he have to commit against my mother and me before we actually—oh, I don't know—*stop forgiving him?* It feels like there should be a specific, quantifiable limit. But I don't know—what's the precise number? There's no handbook or list of rules when dealing with a career-criminal father, is there?" Her voice was wry, but there was real pleading in her tone. "Seriously—*is* there? Inquiring minds are begging."

Now it was my turn to make a face. "*Definitely* don't ask me."

Though I tried not to talk about it, tried to shut it out, the nightmares still haunted me: The Black Hood, aka *my father,* resurrected from the dead for the nth time, looming over the four of us in the woods behind Thistlehouse. An unexpected guest at the world's most macabre dinner party.

Locking eyes with him one last time.

Watching Penelope raise her hand and pull the trigger on her revolver.

The sky, our bones, my skin rattling with an explosion that tore the atmosphere apart.

My father's death was a long time coming, and I could have predicted it would have been a violent one. In the end, it wasn't even all that shocking that I'd been there to witness it myself. Somehow, that aspect of it felt, in the moment, almost fated.

Was I sorry that he was dead? Of course not—if Hiram Lodge was the devil incarnate, my father was evil personified. His darkness was insidious, infectious. As Jughead would say, there was never going to be any redemption arc for him. Death was the only answer.

Was I sorry that he was dead? Of course—he was my *father*. He always would be. Even now, even gone. Even without a chance for that redemption arc that, in my gut, I knew would never have come to bear.

I blinked, pushed away the photo-negative images of Penelope's gun, of my father's body crumpling to the ground. I was getting better at doing that.

It didn't matter, though. No matter how hard I tried to deny the churn of emotions twisting in my gut, V could see them all over my face. She could always see me. That was our friendship, and I was eternally grateful for it.

But I was especially grateful in that moment, when she watched my body language and carefully, without saying anything about my father's death (because really, what was there to say at this point, anyway?), she put an arm around my shoulder and tilted her head against mine. I could smell the rosewater she spritzed on her face when she traveled ("Hydration is key," she liked to say, and she wasn't wrong; her skin was

perpetually flawless, and her beauty tips, infallible). The familiar scent of it was almost as soothing as the warmth of our
shoulders side by side.

Moments like these—with my friends, with Jughead—were
literally the only reason I was starting to keep the gruesome
nightmares of my father (his life *and* his death) at bay. What
would I do without them?

That was something I truly couldn't consider.

A sharp clap of thunder erupted outside, loud enough that it
seemed for a second or two that the bus was wobbling. From
the back of the bus, someone shrieked—high, nervous, trying
to laugh off the moment of obvious genuine fright. I clenched
my hands tight, balled fists at my sides, until the bus stopped
wobbling. In my head or in reality? I wasn't sure.

"Anyway," Veronica said, after a beat. I blinked, snapping
slowly to semi-attention again. "This conversation coupled
with this weather is all too dreary. I, for one, am over it. Let's
not waste even a drop more energy worrying about my father.
For now, at least, we can rest assured that he's behind bars, as
he should be. And he's not going anywhere. No matter how
many cagey letters he sends just to try to rattle me."

I couldn't resist. "No pun intended?"

She laughed. "Definitely not." She sighed. "But yes: Clearly,
his whole purpose in reaching out was to get a rise out of me.
The last thing I should be doing is taking the bait."

"You can't help but be *slightly* on alert, V," I pointed out.

"Maybe you took the bait for a second, okay. But you don't have to keep it."

"Well said, Betty." She settled back into her seat, relaxing and letting her head drop back. "This weekend will be great. We need it—some girl time, out of town and away from it all."

From the back rows of the bus, we heard the first strains of a round of "Ninety-Nine Bottles of Syrup on the Wall," a Riverdale road-trip classic.

"Not quite away from it *all*," I said wryly.

"Well, no. But"—she took my hand—"Vixens! Cheer camp! Team building! Maple s'mores. Come on—even this city sophisticate is excited about that." She grinned. "What could possibly go wrong?"

∧∧∧

The sound was a rumble—deep, hungry—that felt like the earth opening up.

I sat up, confused and panicked, heart hammering against my ribs. Beside me, Veronica's eyes flew open, too, and she grabbed my arm tight enough that I knew that getting into the shower later that night, I would see a perfect imprint of her fingers blooming purple against my skin.

"What's going on?" someone said—screamed, really. Was it me? Veronica? I couldn't tell. *Everyone* was shrieking, shouting, screaming; it was all around us as I slowly woke up to the dawning realization that something truly frightening was going on right now. It was a confusing blur of sound and movement: The bus actually was shaking this time—*that*, I knew for sure—and the panic surrounding me was so sharp that the air around me crackled.

"Holy—!"

Another scream: Ginger, this time, clinging to Tina as tightly as Veronica had grabbed for me. Her face was teary, panicked.

"VIXENS, STAY CALM!" Cheryl shouted, her tinny, high-pitched voice sounding anything but. She was standing, braced against her seat, her tiny, pale frame bouncing as the bus barreled ahead.

"REMAIN IN YOUR SEATS," she yelled, straining to be heard over the chaos and the sounds of the storm raging outside.

"That goes for you, too!" Toni's hand and the very top of her head were visible from behind the seat, her arm reaching up and tugging at Cheryl, imploring her to sit back down.

"That goes for *everyone*!" Coach Grappler's voice was gruff, insistent. She shouted at us over her shoulder, though she obviously didn't dare take her eyes off the road. In the rearview mirror, I could make out her expression. Her face was tight with anxiety, but she was doing her best to keep calm for us. I could see, though, the whites of her knuckles against the blue vinyl of the steering wheel, and I felt a lick of adrenaline spark in my veins.

"Please stay calm and *please* stay seated. You too, Cheryl! We're going to be *fine*—"

She was cut off by a loud *thud* as a—rock? Piece of asphalt? It happened too quickly for me to tell—flew into a window at the front of the bus, shattering a nasty spider's web pattern into the glass. The cracks continued spreading across the glass until—

"Get *down*," Toni shrieked, quickly springing into motion now. She leaped up and covered Cheryl with her own tiny body, smoothly enveloping the both of them inside her windbreaker.

Rain sprayed, confetti-like, through the broken glass.

"Keep your head down!" Veronica yelled, her lips pressed up close against my ear. "There's glass and who knows what else flying around."

The bus reverberated with the deafening sound of a horn, honking long and insistent. It was a truck, a large rig, pulling around us and speeding over the twin yellow lines of the median divider, tearing out past our bus with seemingly zero regard for the storm raging around us. The truck raced off, spraying a fierce shower of rain in its wake. I couldn't help it—I clutched harder at V's hand, hard enough that she squirmed in her seat. She didn't pull away, though.

"It's going to be fine," she tried, but it was a little less convincing now, and her voice had a quaver in it that I couldn't miss. "The storm is—well, I think we'll be okay if we can get around the downed trees . . ."

"*You need to sit!*" Coach Grappler waved frantically with one arm as we swerved across the road again. "The road, it looks floo—"

Her voice cut off.

It looks flooded. That's what Coach Grappler had been trying to say. All it would have taken was another quick glance out the windows to understand that. But we didn't have time to glance out the windows again, not even quickly, not at all, until we were sliding, jointless and smooth as a snake, into the flood zone, feeling the bus quake and the engine roar as Coach Grappler—acting on pure instinct, pure reflex, obviously— did exactly the thing you *aren't* supposed to do when you hydroplane.

She slammed on the brakes.

Of course, it was only later that we realized exactly what had happened. Like I say—in the moment, there wasn't even a beat for us to glance out the window. There wasn't time to do more than register the shiver of our path in the road and the shock on Coach Grappler's face in the vast expanse of the bus's rearview mirror.

Then we were floating, flying, gliding through the tide of the storm.

It looks flooded. That was what she would have said.

If she'd had a chance to, before everything cut to black.

Mercifully, it was quiet at last.

PART TWO:
THE GATHERING STORM

CHAPTER SIX

POP TATE

"A perfect storm brings out the wild."

That's what my mother used to say.

I'd ask, "Whose wild?" and she'd just shrug—it didn't matter; it wasn't about any specific person. It was all of us, and it was everywhere, and thankfully, it didn't happen often.

But that didn't mean that it didn't happen.

My mother was prone to bouts of philosophy. I've always been a bit more pragmatic myself. But there were some things, some times . . . well, let's just say it didn't always matter how reasonable you wanted to pretend to yourself you were. Sometimes, there were things that simply defied reason, and even a pragmatic man had to acknowledge that from time to time.

We've seen some things, my family has. We don't always like to talk about it, but we Tates have been here as long as the town has (and going back, further, to the days before Riverdale was officially recognized on the map). Good, bad . . . you can dredge up every last footnote in our town's layered history, and you can bet the Tates were there to see it.

For better or for worse. Whether we wanted to be there to bear witness or not.

(Ask my mother about the darker side to Riverdale, and she'd go quiet again. Mama didn't like to speak ill if she could avoid it. "Why court darkness?")

Sure, even with all those dark secrets, we had plenty of fun. Still do. There were the handful of celebrities who'd tasted our famous malted milk shakes—including Neil Armstrong (impressive guy, but he tracked mud all over my floor, which made him a little more human to me). Some pop stars who left concert tickets I'd never use in their wake. I passed them along to the waitresses, the youngsters, the ones who were better suited for a loud, late night.

But I was talking about the Wild, as my mother called it, claiming even on her deathbed that she saw figures, was plagued by them. Shadow puppets writing in the distance, just out of sight of the rest of us. Dancing and laughing and weaving their tales, readying for havoc as she prepared to leave this mortal coil, to embrace the endless sleep that comes for us all.

Some of us sooner than later. That was part of the Wild, too. Death haunting us, lingering in the dusty corners and neglected cellars we tried so carefully to sidestep. Creeping after us, always hovering beyond our field of vision.

Like "Sweetie," Riverdale's own Loch Ness monster, spotted by few but blamed by many for a troubling number of vanishings, drownings, and disappearances . . . mostly during summer, when the kids would spend long, sticky days cooling off in Sweetwater River. More than one reporter from out of town had gotten a whiff of that story over the years. And more than one hoity-toity out-of-town reporter had come sniffing around, tape recorder and notebook in hand, hoping for an exposé . . .

Only to disappear themselves. No trace left behind.

It's just Riverdale. Our town, and our Wild. It's innate, a part of our beating heart. It touches us all, colors us all.

Some folks think Jason Blossom was the first body to be found in Sweetwater River. Those are the naïve ones. The ignorant ones.

But maybe they're also the lucky ones. Maybe I'd be happy to trade, given what I know about this town, that river, and all our endless, Wild history.

There was a time, I would have sworn to you, that I once even served a cheeseburger to the devil himself.

Yes, I know how it sounds. And still.

I showed him a kindness at a time when our little Chock'Lit Shoppe was fixing to get run out of business. And let me tell you: Times were tough . . .

And then, just like that . . . they weren't.

A mysterious man came in, and I served him. Wasn't no time after that, business turned around. Hand to heart, that's how it happened. It's not something I'd lie about, and I'm not much one for tall tales.

Did I sell my soul to him? No, of course not. But I do wonder: Would things have happened differently if I'd been different—less friendly, less accommodating—that night?

Would our restaurant still be here? Would I?

But I shouldn't ask questions I don't actually want the answer to. So mostly, I don't dwell. Try not to, at any rate.

We've seen things, the Tates have. All of us. Sasquatch-like mythical creatures (some of which turned out to be all too human, like the Gargoyle King). Dashing men in dark suits with devious intentions behind their eyes. Our town, stalked by the Black Hood. The lingering memory of the horror of the Maple Man; legend or no, his legacy still stained our local lore. One thing we learned from that darkness: It doesn't matter how deep you bury the past, it's always there, lurking, just beneath the surface.

Some of our past, some of the evil, the darkness, it was fixed. Unmoving. Real. You could put a face on it, a name to it. Like Clifford Blossom, putting a bullet in between his own boy's eyes. Like Penelope Blossom, snatched from an orphanage and forced to live first as sister and later as wife. Like poor Betty Cooper, her daddy a serial killer stalking the town, just begging for his daughter to give chase, to dare put a stop to him . . . or maybe join him in his games.

The rain brings out the Wild. That's something I've known to be true.

Riverdale knows darkness, but so do some of our neighbors.

We don't talk about it much, but there've been stories telling of all sorts of madness. Sorcery. Witchcraft. Necromancy. Cannibalism. The sort of dark that goes beyond even what our own small town generally fathoms, that goes beyond our own demons, nightmarish though they are.

The stories come from different places, sure. But none so often as Greendale.

I can't say why. Sometimes these stories, these things . . . they just happen. One incident, then two or three. Suddenly, a town finds that it has a reputation. And though we don't talk about it, Greendale is one of those towns. It's just one of those things everyone knows.

Another legend, quieter this time. Guarded by the girls, passed among friends. Whispered over campfires, repeated in tones of breathless warning in front of the mirror at the bathroom sink. Shared and happily passed from hand to eager hand, like a tube of lipstick or a can of diet pop at a slumber party. They wrap their stories in silk and sugar, keep them tucked away from the eyes and ears of grown-ups . . . But we Tates? We know. We've been here so long—you might say we *are* the town's ears, eyes.

The town's sin-eaters, if you're feeling superstitious.

And these days, I couldn't help but feel that way.

The legend: a young girl, tormented by those who would have been her friends, her peers. (But it's always like that with kids, isn't it? Especially with the girls, so candy-sweet in pictures, but barbed and violent, casually cruel with one another when the camera's turned away.)

"Just pranks," is what they always say. "It was only ever just pranks."

They say it after, of course. After the victim has been pushed too far.

As if "pranks" is enough to cover it. As if it even remotely touches on the shining, rotted face of evil that's been revealed, once the dust has cleared and the damage has all been done. Done, and swept under the rug. Back into our town's dirty footnotes.

As though there's any excuse, any answer or rationalization that could be given.

As if—by the time the story's come to light—it weren't already too late.

"Harmless," they cluck, defensive. "All fun and games."

As if there were any such thing.

As if their fun and games weren't exactly what some people—the wrong people, just the very people we should all be giving a very wide berth—use as flame to their tinderbox, as the perfect storm of humiliation and rage to raise the devil himself.

Or barring that, at least, to raise something Wild.

CHAPTER SEVEN

> ☀ RIVW WEATHER   1 min. ago
>
> Our satellites tell us that our severe storm watch is now in full
> effect, as Riverdale, Greendale, and the immediate surrounding
> areas are all currently experiencing intermittent flash flooding.
> Helicopters report severe conditions on I-95, including several
> downed trees and high waters on local access roads. At this
> time, we are advising drivers to stay off the road until further
> notice. Be smart and stay safe, Riverdale!
>
> —RIVW.com and affiliates

∧∧∧

Jughead:

Hey, Betty, just heard the latest weather report.
Sounds like it's getting hairy out there. (Seems
like it, too, just based on what I can see from
looking out the window.) They're saying flooding
on the highway access roads?

Jughead:

Anyway, I assume your coach wouldn't have
you out there driving if you were really in danger,
so I'm sure it's fine. But text when you get this,
OK? I worry.

Jughead:

Arch, have you heard from the girls?

Archie:

Not in a while. Ronnie was saying she thought cell service would be sketchy the closer they got to the camp.

Jughead:

Makes sense . . . but I don't have to like it.

Archie:

The storm?

Jughead:

Yeah . . .

Jughead:

I'm probably just being paranoid or something. Obviously she wouldn't be out there if it were really dangerous.

Archie:

Right. I mean . . . there are adults who are, like, in charge of these decisions and stuff. So . . .

Ha, yeah. And when have the adults in charge of the "decisions and stuff" in our lives EVER steered us wrong? Or for that matter, into danger?

Archie:

Good point. But try not to stress too badly. They're fine, and I'm sure they'll be in touch as soon as they can. I'll let you know if I hear from them.

Jughead:

Yep, I'll do the same.

∿∿∿

VERONICA

"Betty? *Betty!*"

Concern rose in my voice as I crouched over my best friend. She was splayed across our seats, head against the window. There was no blood, but she was out cold, and had been since the bus careened off the road, which to me spelled concussion. My hands itched to tap her on the shoulder or to shake her ever so gently just to elicit *some* reaction, any sort of reaction, but the little I knew about first aid (which, admittedly, wasn't much) suggested that moving her was the very worst thing I could do. Instead, I hovered over her, anxiety crawling across my skin, waiting for some sign that she was okay.

All around me, other Vixens were doing the same. Coach Grappler was walking up and down the aisle doing a preliminary head count and assessing any injuries. Thankfully, we seemed to have sidestepped anything too major.

Assuming, that was, that Betty was okay. I took a deep breath and forced myself to let it out slowly. Coach Grappler hadn't made her way to us just yet. She was still poring over Cheryl and Toni, confirming that neither had been cut by any shards of glass after the window was broken. A few seats behind them, Ginger patted an antibacterial wipe where she *had* been sliced. It was a superficial wound—it had already stopped bleeding—but the thin trail of red it left along her chiseled cheekbone was unnerving.

"Come on, girl," I begged. I held my hand over Betty's shoulder, fighting the urge to touch her, to feel her warmth under my fingers.

"What happened?"

I let out a huge sigh of relief as Betty's eyelids fluttered open, trying to give her a reassuring smile as her eyes darted around the bus, taking in the scene.

She slowly began to prop herself up on her elbows, confused. Now I *did* lean forward and help her, extending a hand to her for balance. "Did we . . . crash?"

"We skidded off the road," I clarified. "No actual collision, and no one's seriously hurt. Although the front of the bus is pretty banged up, and there are some crazy warning lights going off on the dashboard, or so Coach Grappler says."

Unfortunately, my own familiarity with motor vehicles basically began and ended with Daddy's convertible Jag, which, once upon a time, I was allowed to drive—on special occasions. (Before I put him in prison, that is. Funny how he's touchy about stuff like that.) Auto repair was Betty's department.

"And I was . . . knocked out?" She searched my face for clues with understandably worried eyes. Gently, she started stretching and flexing her limbs, one at a time, tilting her head to one side and then the other, tapping it gingerly—assessing her body for injury, I could see. She winced, twisting at a twinge in her side. "Ouch."

"Briefly," I said, trying to sound reassuring. "We probably need to get you checked out by a medical professional sooner rather than later."

Betty made a face. "That's definitely not necessary. I don't think it's anything major." She shifted again, more gently this time, testing. "Good as new." Her tight smile told me she wasn't *quite* good as new, necessarily—but determined to fake it, anyway.

"I'm glad you've got your can-do Betty Cooper spirit, but you are out of your head *loca* if you think I'm just going to hand wave away what may very well be a concussion."

"It's not," she said, sounding certain.

"You can't be sure," I protested.

"You haven't thrown up, have you?" It was Toni, having sidled into the seat in front of us and peering at Betty now with a quizzical expression.

"No." Betty shook her head.

"That doesn't mean—" I started.

"No," Toni agreed, "it definitely doesn't mean anything for certain. But I've seen enough concussions from back-alley brawls during my barback days at the Whyte Wyrm to know that if she hasn't thrown up and isn't having vision problems or a headache, even if she does have a concussion, it's probably mild."

"Strangely, that's not as comforting as I suspect you were intending it to be," I said, trying not to sound snappish. Toni was just trying to help, but this was my bestie—I didn't want to take chances.

"Veronica," Toni said, putting a hand on my shoulder, "the thing is, if it *is* a concussion, all we do is watch it. She can take an ibuprofen if her head hurts."

"*She* is sitting right here," Betty reminded us, sounding a little irked but obviously trying to stay patient and calm. "And V, if there's no actual treatment for a concussion, then what's the point of . . . I don't even know, jeopardizing everyone else on the bus, trying to drive to some random hospital in the middle of nowhere for some kind of confirmation that won't help or change anything?"

I folded my arms across my chest. "I don't like this."

She gestured outside, past the windows, where rain crashed down in gray, insistent sheets, and branches and other detritus danced across the road with the wind. "I don't like *this*. This storm is what we *really* need to be worried about. So the sooner we stop worrying about me and start worrying about our next steps, the better."

"The storm? Purely a swirl of meaningless sound and fury." Cheryl floated over to us, snuggling up to Toni with a smug smile. Impossibly, her matte Red Velvet lipstick was still flawless.

"Fear not, dear cousin. As Veronica says, despite our unfortunate near collision, all Vixens are present, accounted for, and mostly in one piece." She leaned closer, conspiratorial. "Tina's got a goose egg on her forehead that's got to smart. And Ginger has that ugly scrape that we pray won't leave a scar. But truly, that seems to be the worst of it. Even my own delicate porcelain skin remains largely unmarred by bruising, a gift from the Goddess herself." She held out her arms to show me just how pristine and unbruised her skin was.

"Still, though. Betty *was*—"

"I. Am. Okay." Betty smirked at me.

Fine, maybe she *was* okay. She was certainly looking better— rosier cheeks, brighter eyes—as the minutes ticked by. But I *still* wanted her to get a quick once-over from someone who knew more than we did. If I knew my girl, she was going to brush off her little minor trauma and get right back to business. That was Betty's MO: one foot in front of the other, always wanting to do the right thing, the "normal" thing. The thing that meant she was just like every other average teenager, as opposed to a ticking time bomb whose very DNA was possibly tainted by a serial killer's genes.

That was why she needed her bestie—to ensure that she take a beat and tend to herself.

"Yes, Veronica," Cheryl said, rolling her eyes. "We did hear you the first time. Wherefore the histrionics, cousin?" She shot Betty a look. "Has that iconic ponytail of yours been knocked off-center in all the hubbub?"

Betty held her hands up—*not me*. "No histrionics. My hair's fine. *I'm* fine."

"Which we all know is your standard party line," I cut in. "We love you for that indomitable spirit. And I'm sure it's the truth. But I, for one, would still feel better if you got looked at by, you know, a medical professional. Honestly—we probably all should. Where's the harm, right? Better safe than sorry."

Cheryl shrugged. "To each her high-maintenance own."

I resisted the urge to laugh. As if that weren't the Prada tote calling the Lululemon yoga pants black, as it were.

"Thanks, Cheryl. It's very generous of you to allow me the privilege of my own opinion." There was no mistaking the sarcastic undertones to my comment. I squeezed Betty's hand.

"I've got you, girl. I'll just talk to Coach Grappler, figure out what's going on. Be right back."

I shimmied out of our seat and made my way to where Coach Grappler was, waving those single-sheet antibacterial wipes like a magician fanning out a deck of cards. The broken window was letting in biting gusts of wind and spatters of rain that kicked up in intensity every few minutes. Around me, despite Cheryl's insistence that all was well, the Vixens looked startled, shaken.

Coach Grappler was flustered, her face a bright pink and a tiny crown of frizz rising from her hairline. It was a stark contrast to how poised she generally looked, just in the short amount of time I'd spent with her. She'd given up her windbreaker to someone who'd been caught under the broken window, so her shirt was soaked through, and up close, I could see the raised gooseflesh on her arms. A bruise in the shape of the curve of the steering wheel arced angrily across her collarbone.

"Coach," I said, "Cheryl says you're reporting no one is hurt. And, the girls do look fine, overall. But Betty might have a concussion . . ." I gestured, but her expression stayed impassive, which was admittedly unnerving, even to someone as difficult to intimidate as me.

I pushed forward, determined and undeterred. "It's just that I think we should probably see a medic sooner rather than later. It feels like the prudent course of action. I'm sure you agree."

"Veronica Lodge," Coach said. She scanned me appraisingly. We hadn't had much time together since the meeting to announce this retreat (and certainly not one-on-one); I could only imagine what opinions she'd formed of me based solely on the rumors on which our town thrived. *Mobster's daughter. Both parents incarcerated. Her father, for the second time—and surely not his last.*

And she didn't even know about all the times my parents had tried to have each other killed.

Was I ashamed of my family history? Absolutely not. My parents' transgressions are theirs alone, and Veronica Lodge answers to no one, after all. But this woman was our new coach, and who knew how much time we'd be spending together over the course of the year? I wanted to get off on the right foot, it's true. So sue me.

(JK, obvi. More litigation is literally the last thing I need in my life.)

But yes, Veronica Lodge is—generally speaking—used to making a stellar first impression, and I didn't want this particular moment to be the exception to the rule.

"The one and only," I said.

"Principal Honey told me to look to you as a girl who gets things done."

"Principal Honey knows of what he speaks." Score one for another good first impression, then.

"I'm glad you think so," she said. "It just so happens that I agree with you. The girls need some triage, something a little better than I can do here on the bus. So we're on the same page there."

"Excellent," I said. "Though I'm sensing a *but* coming up."

She frowned. "Well. The good news is I'm certified in first aid. And when we get to camp, I can give everyone a good once-over."

"What's the bad news?" I asked, wary. "Are we *able* to get to camp with the storm? And the damage to the bus?"

She made a face. "That's the *but*, as you say. It's . . . well, it's probably better if I just let everyone know, all together." She gestured for me to step back, clearing the way for her to move to the aisle so she could address the group.

"Vixens," she began, standing tall and projecting out, all the way toward the back of the bus despite the sound of thrashing rainfall through the broken window. Standing next to her, I watched as the girls all swiveled, eyes on Coach Grappler, at attention. The air was thick with nerves and not a little bit of real fear.

"As some of you have realized, the bus was damaged when we swerved off the road. Thankfully, no one's been seriously hurt—though I'm going to be giving everyone a more thorough examination once we get to Sweetwater Pines. That's, ah . . . that's the good news, as I've been saying to Veronica here."

A flurry of relieved murmurs swept across the group as everyone's eyes skated from Coach Grappler to me.

"The bad news," she went on, "is that one of the head-lights is shattered, and there's definitely something else going on with the engine. We're actually not that far from the camp, but it's going to be a while before we make it there. It would be dangerous to drive with the busted headlight in this weather, not to mention illegal. I radioed for Triple B, but given the storm, I'm thinking it will be a long wait. So my suggestion to you is to fish what you can out of your luggage to help you stay warm and dry, and hunker down. We may as well get comfortable."

There was a collective groan as everyone took this in. "Did Triple B even give an ETA for how long it would be?" Tina called out. I glanced at her; Cheryl hadn't been exaggerating about the bump on her forehead. She definitely went to the front of the line for a thorough exam—right behind Betty.

Coach shook her head. "It's pretty messy out there. We're not the only ones who need help, and our situation is much less urgent than some others."

"That's a matter of opinion," Cheryl snapped. "That being said, you're all delusional if you think I'm waiting around for an eternity just for some jumpsuit-clad grease monkeys to arrive on scene and rescue us like a pack of swooning damsels in distress."

Beside her, Toni snickered. And, credit where credit was due, I had to hand it to Cheryl—we all knew she was nobody's damsel.

Now it was Coach Grappler's turn to sigh. "Okay," she said. "In that case, what would you suggest? Since I can't *make* the mechanics move any faster than they'll move."

"No, I suppose you can't," Cheryl agreed. "You're only human. And more's the pity. But as it happens, Toni and I overheard you consorting with Triple B just after the crash."

Betty caught my eye and flashed me an incredulous look. *Consorting?* she mouthed, shaking her head. I stifled a giggle.

If Coach Grappler was also incredulous, she did a truly commendable job of hiding it. "Is that right?"

"It's true," Toni chimed in. "I mean, not that we were eavesdropping—"

"Speak for yourself, my beloved," Cheryl said. "Personally, I see no shame in staying informed."

"Okay, whatever." Toni would always be as sanguine about Cheryl's . . . inane *Cheryl*ness as anyone. Which made sense given their status as OTP. "The point is, we heard you guys talking. And we know we're basically *at* Sweetwater Pines. Like, walking distance to the grounds."

"That's . . . true," Coach Grappler said, careful. "Meaning *what,* exactly?"

"Meaning that, to paraphrase another badass bombshell herself, one Nancy Sinatra: These cherry-red rain boots were made for walking. As in, they were literally hand-designed for me. And that's just what I propose we do."

Now *I* was the incredulous one. "You want us to walk to the camp? In this storm?" I asked.

"Oh, Veronica. Ever the fragile flower. Have some Vixen moxie, woman! The sooner we get to the camp, the sooner we can shower—albeit, in more rustic environs than I generally prefer—and the sooner we can cozy up to some dry clothes. I, for one, have some crimson cashmere joggers simply calling to me from my duffel bag."

Coach Grappler looked highly skeptical. "Think this through, Cheryl. I'm responsible for your safety."

Cheryl snorted. "With all due respect, Coach Grappler, this is Riverdale. Those of us with parents who aren't woefully negligent have been straight-up physically or emotionally endangered by them. No one will put up a fuss if we take a short stroll in the rain to get to a school-sanctioned event. Even if we're briefly unchaperoned."

"Hard to believe though that may be, it's the truth," I said. Betty nodded somberly, too.

Coach Grappler appeared to be thinking this over. "Okay, I hear you. Although we're definitely going to come back to that later. Still . . . is *anyone* getting any cell service? I used the radio for Triple B, but I'm getting nothing on my phone."

Across the bus, a sea of dubious Vixens shook their heads in unison.

"Cell service, no," Toni said. "But GPS works just fine.

I can see the camp on my phone, no problem, and I've mapped the route."

Betty maneuvered her way out of her seat and moved up to Toni. "May I?" she asked, reaching for the phone. Once Toni had handed it over, she ran her index finger over the screen, presumably scanning the map.

When she was finished, she looked up. "Honestly?" she said, looking at me though she faced the rest of the group. "She's right. It's totally doable, especially since we have GPS."

"Okay," I said. I trusted my girl. "But real talk: How accurate is GPS in the woods? I mean, there aren't any roads to follow between here and camp, are there?"

"Actually, there are," Betty said. She passed the phone to me so I could have a look. "We're not that far from the exit to the local road for the camp. There are only a few tiny turns that *might* take us into the woods on our way."

"*Might?*" Ginger echoed, her voice shaky and shrill. She glanced at the window, as though if she just concentrated hard enough, she'd be able to control the weather with her mind.

"Guys." Betty smiled, calm. "I promise you, it's nothing. I was an Adventure Scout from kindergarten through sixth grade, and believe me when I tell you: I earned *all* the merit badges."

"And while we all know that Betty Cooper doesn't come to play," I said, stepping in, "I'd be remiss if I didn't take the opportunity to voice my own concerns."

Lowering my voice slightly, I said, "B, I don't doubt your navigational skills for a moment. You know I'd trust you with my life. But are you sure we're not better off waiting on the mechanics?"

"Since when has *waiting around* ever been our thing?" she pointed out.

Touché.

"You have a point," I admitted.

"Of course she does," Cheryl chimed in, smirking at me. "Congratulations on finally seeing the light of reason." She looked at the rest of the Vixens, all utterly captivated by her.

"All in favor of taking destiny into our own hands and not wasting another precious second on this pathetically run-down vehicle?" She gestured, though she hardly needed to. Rain still sluiced rhythmically through the broken window, and most of us were waterlogged and shivering.

The truth was, Cheryl's decision had already been made. The vote itself was clearly moot. More a show of solidarity than anything else.

But take it from a mobster's daughter: Solidarity counted for something. I looked at Betty, communicating in our own secret, silent best-friend code. She nodded. Slowly, we both raised our hands. One by one, the rest of the Vixens followed suit.

Coach Grappler's expression was inscrutable, but the masses had spoken. And as we'd all learned the hard way at one point or another, when Cheryl Blossom got an idea into her pretty little head? Well, resistance was pretty much futile.

"Okay," Coach said, her shoulders slumping ever so slightly, "since you *do* have GPS, and we *are* very close to the camp—"

"Barely two miles, as per this map," Cheryl said. "To be precise."

"Yes, that would constitute 'very close,' as I said," Coach Grappler went on. Her patience for Cheryl (and maybe the entire, messy situation as a whole) was clearly wearing thin. "So, given that, you can walk to the camp. As long as you *stick together*. I'll wait for the mechanics, and I'll get to the camp as soon as possible. Who knows? Maybe they'll miraculously be quicker than I'm expecting."

"Who knows, indeed?" Cheryl echoed, bright. But she'd clearly moved on from Coach and the entire issue of the stranded bus.

"Compatriots," she said, her voice ringing loudly, "you have ten minutes to gather your essentials into your backpacks. Then we head off."

That seemed abrupt, even given the legitimate direness of our situation. I held up a hand. "*Ten* mi—"

She ignored me, pushing forward. "Betty Cooper is our navigator. I trust we all feel comfortable with that?" Everyone murmured their assent. At least she was ceding some minuscule aspect of her power, I thought. Putting Betty in charge of navigation showed an awareness of the realities of our situation. Thank goodness.

"Cousin?" Cheryl said, looking at Betty. "Even with a mild concussion, surely you're the most capable of our crew, I'll admit."

"I'm happy to lead," Betty said.

"*Navigate*," Cheryl corrected. "*I'll* be leading."

"Sure, yes. *Navigate*." Betty rolled her eyes.

"Perfect!" Cheryl squealed. She clapped her hands together, the sharp, bloodred tips of her manicure dancing in the air, far lighter and airier than our moods were. "*Parfait*. It's all settled. Off we go!" She beamed, then went stern again. "Chop-chop! Ten minutes and counting!"

With that, we all sprang into action.

CHAPTER EIGHT

Alice Cooper:

Jughead, have you heard from Betty?

Jughead:

Mrs. Cooper! Hey. How are you?

Alice Cooper:

I'm fine. Betty? Have you heard anything from her?

Jughead:

Sorry, yeah. No, I haven't. Not since the Vixens left for Sweetwater Pines. Why? Did something happen?

Alice Cooper:

Well, no . . . not yet.

Jughead:

Sorry?

Alice Cooper:

I mean, not that I know of. But I'm here at the station. We're covering the storm watch, and it looks like the roads are in pretty bad shape.

Alice Cooper:

Honestly, the Vixens should have just rescheduled the trip. But if they're already on their way, the least they could do is to keep in touch and let a worried mother know that everything's fine.

Jughead:

I know, I've been texting, but I'm not hearing back.

Alice Cooper:

I can't say that's very reassuring.

Jughead:

I know. But try to keep calm. That's what I'm doing, anyway. If nothing else, keep in mind who we're dealing with here. It's BETTY. That girl can handle herself.

Alice Cooper:

I know you mean well, Jughead. But I'm her mother. You're out of your mind if you think I'm going to be placated with that meaningless platitude, no matter how well intentioned it may be. No offense.

Jughead:

Right. None taken.

Alice Cooper:

If you do talk to her, let her know to call me. As soon as possible.

Jughead:

Of course. Have a good one.

Alice Cooper:

I doubt that very much.

Jughead:

Fair enough, Mrs. Cooper. Talk to you later.

∼∼∼

Jughead:

Dad, you around?

FP Jones:

I've got a minute. What's going on, boy?

Jughead:

Just a heads-up that I just heard from Betty's mom and she's . . . a little frantic. To put it mildly. Really worried about Betty and the Vixens out there in this weather.

FP Jones:

Oh, you think so?

Jughead:

I take it you've already heard from her.

FP Jones:

Just a few times, yeah.

Jughead:

So then you know. OK. I was gonna ask you to maybe check in, keep an eye on her and stuff. But I guess you're on top of it.

FP Jones:

You're thinking like a gentleman. I like it. But don't worry, like you say—I'm already all over this. I got it. So if you talk to Betty, and she tells you she heard from her mom and her mom's being a little, well . . .

Jughead:

If she says her mom's being a little, well, HER MOM . . . Only, even more so—if that's even possible.

FP Jones:

Exactly. And yeah—it's possible. Trust me. Anyway, if you hear from her, just let Betty know I'm keeping an eye on Alice. I'll do my best to rein her in.

Jughead:

Great, will do.

FP Jones:

Anything else?

Jughead:

Well, actually, since you ask . . .

Jughead:

Do you think the Vixens are safe? In the storm?

FP Jones:

Come on now, boy. I know you and your friends think the grown-ups in this town don't know our behinds from our elbows, but I promise you, no one from the school board would send any of you out on the road in a storm if there were any real danger. Not after everything that happened with the Fizzle Rocks and the seizures. Every now and then the people in this town DO learn our lesson. Riverdale can't take another incident like that.

Jughead:

Fair. But I'd feel a lot more soothed if I hadn't already heard that song about a million times before.

FP Jones:

Come on, boy. It'll be fine. Besides—
it's BETTY. That girl can handle herself.

Jughead:

Huh.

FP Jones:

Huh, what?

Jughead:

It's just . . . Mrs. Cooper was right. That
platitude really ISN'T as comforting as I
would have thought.

Jughead:

On the other hand, you and I do have more in
common than might immediately meet the eye.

FP Jones:

Now you're talking in riddles. No matter. I'll
check in with you later. Stay out of the storm.

Jughead:

I will. Ttyl. ☺

FP Jones:

Since when do you text like your kid sister?

Jughead:

Here I thought I was taking a page from your playbook, Old Man.

FP Jones:

?

FP Jones:

Gotta run. See you back home later. Be careful out there.

∿∿

REGGIE

"So, this place went mega high-tech last year for Veronica's casino night. She basically runs everything off a BuyPad, and the devices are all smart."

I led the way through La Bonne Nuit, with Jughead and Archie following close at my heels. The two of them were like a golden retriever and a grumpy little junkyard mutt, slinking around and sniffing at everything, curious and kind of cautious, too. Holding up the tablet so they'd get a good look, I tapped the control that hit the overhead lights. Suddenly La Bonne Nuit was brighter than a shopping mall in the afternoon. All yellow fluorescent and industrial-like. It was a weird vibe, even for someone like me who spent lots of off-hours here cleaning, stocking, and generally looking after the place when it's not open and operating as Riverdale's number one nightlife hot spot.

Honestly, though? Dope as the speakeasy was, it wasn't like there was so much competition in our town, hot spot–wise. Which is probably how Ronnie knew this place would be such a success in the first place. Girl's got a head for business—it was one of her father's rare good qualities—and she'd been putting that skill to good use for as long as I'd known her.

Man. Smart *and* gorgeous . . . I'd be lying if I said it didn't still bug me that she chose Archie over me. All the more reason kicking his ass tonight at poker was going to feel that much sweeter.

"Yeah, I remember how it works," Archie said. But he looked confused, so I knew he didn't, not totally.

Good, I thought. Yeah, he had Ronnie. But in this case, *I* had the upper hand.

"It's in . . ." He scratched his head. "You just go to the—"

"You go to the settings app," I said, mercifully cutting him off. "You can also program voice activation, if you wanted to bypass the tablet completely. But that's, like, next-level. We can stick to the basics tonight." I smirked. *Basic.* That was a good word for Andrews, all right.

"Weren't there all those false doors and things that would come down? At the press of a button?" Jughead asked. "It was like a whole *Guys and Dolls* thing—with about the same amount of theatrics, if memory serves."

"Yeah," I said. "Ronnie had all that stuff installed in case of a raid. That girl doesn't take chances."

"And she put in a camera system, too," Archie said. "State of the art. She piggybacked onto the wiring system that was put in for all those false fronts and stuff. She told me all about it. She's been nagging me to put one in at the community center, ever since Dodger and his crew started coming around, but I haven't had a chance yet."

"Yeah," I said, annoyed. "Lots of toys. Practically Batwoman."

I needed to change the subject without making it seem like I was *trying* to change the subject. The good news was: My boy Andrews really wasn't the sharpest tool in the shed. And overall, he was *way* too trusting.

The bad news? Jughead Jones was exactly the opposite. And right now, he was scanning the speakeasy like he was trying to memorize its schematics for a prison break or something. That guy was too nosy for his own good.

"Lots of cameras," I went on, trying to sound casual. "All through this one tiny tablet. It's like something out of a spy movie. But, I mean, it's, like, overkill, man. We don't need *any* surveillance tonight, really. This is just a friendly game of poker. It's not a back room in Vegas." I was pushing this theory hard.

Jughead took a deep breath. He stuffed his hands into his jeans pockets. "Yeah, well, if there's one thing I've learned, it's that there's really no such thing as too much surveillance. Unless we're talking about 'the Man,' like companies data-mining your personal info from your Spacebook page."

"Dude, paranoid much?" *What. A. Freak.*

He just shrugged. "And besides—our 'friendly little game of poker' has basically spiraled to gargantuan proportions. To be honest, this game *may* as well be Vegas. It's not the chill little guys night we first talked about."

"And that's a bad thing?" I ribbed him. "Need I remind you that the more people who come to the game, the bigger the pot? Or are you all set for scratch these days up at your fancy new boarding school?"

He paused. *Bingo.* I had him there. I knew Jughead would be struggling to keep up with the rich douches at Stonehouse, or whatever that place was called. The look on his face—a little shake of his chin while his jaw clenched tight, the red in his cheeks—told me I'd hit a nerve. *Well, good.* That's what I'd wanted to do. That was the whole damn point.

"So, what other toys did Veronica have installed in here?" Jughead said. Now *he* was trying to change the subject . . . unfortunately, to the exact topic I was trying to steer them both away from.

"Dual-authentication–factor ID on the safe," I said, brusque. "And all her smart devices are connected and stuff. So she gets, like, push notifications on her BuyPhone if there's a breach of security or if something random goes wrong with the system."

"Yeah," Jughead said, picking up a router that was tucked behind the bar and examining it as if he were a crime scene investigator or something. "Funny, though—these smart devices are all well and good until your Wi-Fi goes down. Then you've lost everything in one fell swoop. And you're, like, a total slave to the cloud. Betty and I've learned that the hard way with some of our investigations."

"Yeah, I guess," I said. I really didn't want to dwell on any of this. Not right now, and *definitely* not with Jughead scanning the whole place like he was auditioning for a part on *Law & Order: High School Loser Unit*.

I moved behind the bar to take the router from Jughead and to start laying out prep for drinks. I needed to think about how best to set up seating. With a few different card tables, we could have multiple games going. Although the baller game would be at *one* table, obviously. *My* table.

Setting 'em up, knocking 'em down. *Me*, crushing it.

That, I could do.

"Look," I said. "I think it makes sense to set up one large table in the middle of the room. Move the rest of the tables out, spread them around for spectators who want to watch the action while they wait to get in on it. Might be good for building anticipation—and intimidation—too." Bonus.

"That's in addition to the other tables for the smaller-stakes games."

"And, let me guess: You want us to move the tables," Archie said.

I shrugged, glancing at Archie. "I mean, yeah, bro. I'm gonna help, obviously—"

"Oh, obviously," Jughead said, raising an eyebrow.

"Come on, Jug," Archie said. Always the peacekeeper, that one. Some folks said it was what made him such a good guy. But to me, it was what made him a sucker. "Reggie'll help set it up. He knows this place inside and out."

"Like the back of my hand." I smirked. "So, you know I'll help with the tables, but first I need to get all the security stuff up and running. And there's one other crucial step." One of my favorite speakeasy-related tasks.

"What's that?" Archie said curiously, not aggro or suspicious.

Now *I* raised an eyebrow. "Settin' up the bar, bro."

Archie smiled, a big goofy grin that split his pale, freckled face in two. "Right, of course. The bar is definitely your domain. We'll start on the tables, and you can jump in when you're done."

I offered up a quick fist bump. "It's a plan, bro."

"Oh, and, Reggie?" Archie added, calling after me as I moved down to the end of the bar.

"Yeah?"

"Ronnie said not to be shy. Like, we should use the top-shelf stuff, the good stuff, if we want. I mean, it doesn't matter to me, but she was pretty clear about it. *Treat yourself, Archiekins.*" He laughed a little, to himself. "You know how she gets."

Yeah. I do. My jaw tightened, and I clenched my fists at my sides. I *did* know how Ronnie got, and man—*I* got her, too. It was why we were so perfect for each other. The reformed bad girl and the misunderstood prankster? We were meant for each other.

Archie Andrews, on the other hand? What did Ronnie even see in him? What could she possibly want with that strawberry milk shake of a man? Not a man, even—just a boy.

I mean, I know everyone said he'd changed, he was darker, more haunted. He'd come back different after his time in Leopold and Loeb, fighting a bear, and, worst of all, losing his dad. (I mean, I couldn't even imagine, and I didn't even *like* my own old man.) All that crazy, awful crap that had happened to him in the last year that had forced him to grow up too fast.

Okay, so maybe he wasn't a milk shake anymore. But he still wasn't good enough for Veronica Lodge.

I blinked, coming out of that little trance I'd gone into, and realized I'd been staring off in space for a second or two too long. Archie was looking at me like I'd suddenly grown another head or something. I forced a grin. "Yeah, no problem, man," I said. "Top shelf for the top dawgs tonight. You got it."

Archie's phone buzzed, and he reached into his pocket to get it. "Jug," he called, "it's Sweet Pea. He's been trying to get in touch with you. Some Serpents are in town, just passing through, but I guess they wanted to know if they could buy in to tonight's game, too?"

Jughead gave a heavy sigh. "The more the merrier, I suppose," he said. He looked off wistfully. "Remember way back when, when tonight was just going to be quality time for you and me while I was home from school? Those were the days."

"That was *yesterday*," Archie teased. "Hardly, like, a simpler time, man."

"Archie, you wound me. I mean, I know it's aggressively on-brand for Jughead Jones to be so deeply misanthropic . . . but I can't help who I am."

"You *could* work a little harder to hide it, bro," I said, an edge creeping into my tone. I shrugged. I just didn't *get* why this guy wore the whole "I'm a weirdo" thing with such *pride*. "I'm just saying."

"Reggie, Reggie, Reggie . . ." he said. "We're living in the age of authenticity. I gotta be me." He looked at his phone and frowned. "And I *gotta* get a hold of JB before I can even begin to deal with the Serpents and whoever else."

"Is JB doing okay? What's she up to lately?" Archie called,

his voice straining a little bit under the weight of a stack of chairs he was hauling.

"Meaning, since Mom left?" Jughead asked. "*Okay* would be the word for it, I guess. Mostly *not* meeting me where and when she says she will, so that I'm constantly in a state of low-key panic. I mean, I sympathize with her. Her mom *left*. I know exactly what that's like, and it's gotta be worse for a pre-teen girl. But my heart can't take the anxiety." His eyes went wide as something occurred to him. "Crap—is this what our parents feel like all the time? Because if so, maybe an apology or two is in order."

From behind the bar, I tried not to roll my eyes. *Not mine*, I thought.

I mean, he'd never said as much in so many words, but just based on my old man's behavior alone, I had to believe he was way happier when I was out of sight and out of mind. Whenever I *did* manage to catch his attention . . .

Well, let's just say, whenever I did catch his attention, I often ended up wishing I never had in the first place.

∿∿∿

It was Mantle Automotives' anniversary, and my pops had decided to do it up, make a whole thing of the event. A party with refreshments, entertainment . . . as much swag as you could possibly cram into a party for a car dealership in a Podunk place like Riverdale.

(I know, I know: It wasn't saying much. But we were trying.)

Maybe once upon a time, Josie and the Pussycats would have been the go-to pop stars for a bash like this one. But the Pussycats had disbanded, and now Josie was gone. Oh well. Riverdale's loss was my big-time gain. I found Veronica on the football field one afternoon, finishing up Vixens practice around the same time the Bulldogs were packing it in. The timing was good . . . I wanted to look casual, like I hadn't been planning to approach her all along.

"Reggie!" Veronica didn't seem all that surprised to see me next to her, which I took as a good (enough) sign. Her face was flushed and slightly shiny from practice, and when she gathered up her glossy hair into a messy ponytail off her neck, it made me crazy. But I had to be cool.

"I've been meaning to talk to you," I said, like the idea had just this second crossed my mind.

"What about?" She smiled.

"Well, I don't know if you'd heard, but my dad's having this huge party at the dealership next week. You know, for the anniversary."

"I didn't realize," she said. "But that's great news. Kudos to Mantle the senior on a successful, thriving business enterprise."

She was being polite, I could tell. Kids in our school had different ideas about my dad, how they felt about him. Around the time we were all playing G and G, it came out that once in a while he'd give me a shove or two. No big deal, you know? Most people in town chose to look away, if they noticed at all. But not everyone. Not Veronica and her cheesy little group of bleeding-heart pals.

I guess I didn't need her to full-on *like* my dad, though. Or even respect him. Really I just needed her to tolerate him enough to go along with what I was about to propose.

"Thriving, yeah." I nodded. "He added a whole new lot, too. It's the biggest dealership on the Eastern seaboard now. And the party will be filled with starched shirts that need to be impressed. So, naturally, I thought of you. What would you say to a performance?"

"You want me to sing?" She looked more surprised than I would have thought, given that the girl was no stranger to the spotlight. She'd performed with the Pussycats dozens of times in their heyday, and she sang at her speakeasy on the regular.

"The guest list is total pedigree," I said. "It would be great exposure for the speakeasy—and fun!"

She held up a hand. "I'm flattered, Reggie," she said. "It no doubt would be fun. And as a businesswoman, I never turn down free publicity. I'm just not sure if it's a good time . . ."

"The open bar will be off the chain," I put in, trying to stave off what felt like the mother of all "thanks, but no thanks" coming my way.

"It sounds amazing," she said, her voice warm. "But you know I don't drink when I'm performing—or working—anyway."

"Forget the bar," I said, trying to keep the desperate edge from creeping into my voice. "Do it for old times' sake?"

She looked me straight in the eye, her expression softening. *Bingo.* That was the emotion I needed to see.

She sighed. "Oh, Reggie. You do know how to invoke my sense of nostalgia." She shook her head, thinking it over. "Okay. For old times' sake. And all those not-so-old times you helped me out at the speakeasy—even when it wasn't your job."

"Oh, my dad can pay you," I assured her. "Five grand."

Her eyes widened. "Normally, I'd refuse outright," she said. "But that money could go a long way toward helping get Archie's community center off on the right foot. I'll ask him to accompany me. A better show for your party, and he'll be more inclined to take the money from me if he earns at least some of it himself."

Archie. Ouch. Just hearing how his name was the first place her mind went? It was a dagger in my gut.

I had one more card to play before this conversation was over, though. "Great," I said, forcing a smile past gritted teeth. "How about we head to Pop's now—go over the details over a milk shake? Double chocolate—your favorite."

She frowned, glancing quickly at her watch. "Much as I would love that, I promised Archie I'd grab a bite with him." She looked at me, uncertain. "You could come with us." Like we didn't both know how awkward that would be.

"Nah, thanks, though. Wouldn't want to bore him with our shop-talk," I said, shrugging it off. "Another time."

∧∧∧

On the morning of the party, I woke nervous as hell—Pops does *not* like when things don't go according to his own particular vision. And if I wanted to impress Veronica, I needed to keep my dad's temper on ice. So, from the second I peeled my eyes open in bed, my nerves were jangling like I'd accidentally downed four Red Bulls before hitting the cardio circuit at the gym.

The good news was, when I got to the party, everything was already smoothly under way. No hiccups with decor or catering, and even the weather was cooperating—the skies were overcast, but no rain, and the air was warm for the season. The lot was packed with stuffy grown-ups in their business-casual best, a kinda depressing sight for someone as young, hot, and virile as yours truly, but since it was what my dad had wanted, I knew it was a good thing.

I'd arranged for a temporary stage to be put up, and I met Ronnie—*and Archie, ugh*—at the makeshift backstage, where a few scrims were set up to create dressing areas and a thick red curtain had been hung.

"Reggie, man," Archie said, tuning his guitar with his forehead all wrinkled. "Do these people even want entertainment? They look pretty . . . uh, somber."

"Relax," I said, waving a hand. "They're just, you know, adults. A little serious, is all. But that's where you guys come in. You bring joy to the joyless."

Or so I hoped.

Like, really, *really* hoped.

I stepped through the curtains and walked up to the mic, trying to tap into that Mantle swagger. *Please get pumped. please get pumped.* The prayer echoed in my brain as I surveyed the crowd. Archie had nailed it: somber AF, even clutching their overflowing glasses of wine. *Crap.* What if this had been a huge mistake?

"Ladies and gentlemen," I started, my throat catching a little until I coughed to clear it. "Thanks so much for joining us to celebrate the anniversary of the northern Hudson Valley's preeminent automotive dealership: Mantle Automotive."

The group murmured some vague, mildly enthusiastic reply. It was better than nothing, so I charged ahead. "Now put your hands together for Veronica Lodge and—Archie Andrews!"

Okay, so sue me. I choked for a second on Archie's name. Happens to the best of us. Anyway, I recovered.

Luckily the curtains parted and Veronica moved toward me, smooth and graceful as always. She took the mic from me and gestured to Archie as he settled onto his stool and began to strum. Still applauding, I moved off the stage to give her—*them*—their moment.

Attagirl, I thought, watching and admiring as Veronica owned the stage. Her voice was silk, and her face was serene as she gave herself over to the music. It was . . . magic, almost. Like so much so that I could almost forget that the person she was sharing the stage with was *Archie*.

I wasn't the only one who thought it was a home run, either. Two songs in, Dad sidled up to me, red-cheeked from one too many drinks and wobbling slightly. Normally, I'd be wary of him in tipsy mode, but he was grinning so wide I knew I'd aced it.

"My boy," he said, patting me on the shoulder roughly. "You did it. I'm impressed."

"Thanks," I said.

I didn't want to feel that ping in my stomach that told me it mattered, Pops being proud of me. But not wanting it didn't make that feeling go away.

∿∿∿

After her set, I grabbed Veronica "backstage" again. "Congrats, superstar," I said. "That was amazing!" I looked around. "Where'd your boy disappear to?"

"Oh, he went to snag some canapés and I think take a phone call from his mom," Veronica said. "But we both thought it went well! It was a good crowd, Reggie. I commend you."

I peeled off the cash I'd promised. "Your compensation. Don't spend it all in one place . . ." I trailed off, the joke feeling less funny when it hit me that, of course, it would all be going to one place: *Archie's* place.

"Not too shabby for an afternoon's work," she said. "Thanks for thinking of us. This money will do some real good."

She tilted her head, and for a moment I could feel some of our old heat, that undeniable spark—never mind that Andrews was probably no more than twenty feet away.

I wasn't giving up. I'd definitely raise the issue of a celebratory milk shake again. Maybe not right this second—spark or no, I could see the timing wasn't great. But it would happen. And sooner rather than later.

"Anytime," I said, hoping she could hear in my voice all the things I wasn't saying.

Before she could respond, though, the moment was shattered.

"Reginald! Hey! REGINALD!"

It was my father—obviously several drinks further in, judging from how unsteady he was on his feet. His face was red as a tomato now, and sweaty, too; his tie was loosened and he'd pushed his shirtsleeves up. Whatever he was drinking, it was sloshing over the side of the glass he clutched as he made his way over. *Crap.*

He staggered over to us, stumbling against Veronica as he approached and grabbing her roughly by the shoulder to steady himself. "Reginald!" he boomed again, once he'd regained his footing. "I hope you're going to introduce me to this ravishing creature, the likes of which I've never seen!"

I cringed. "Uh . . . yeah. But, Dad, you've met Veronica Lodge, haven't you?" He wasn't big on school functions, but this couldn't be the first time they were coming face-to-face.

"Nice to see you, Mr. Mantle," Veronica said smoothly, shaking his hand and working to diffuse any tension.

"It is nice to meet me, isn't it?" Dad asked, slurring his words.

He gave her a creepy once-over, grinning in a way that made me nauseous. "But it's even nicer to meet an outstanding piece of . . . *ahem, performer* . . . such as yourself."

Gross. The old man practically had his tongue hanging out of his mouth.

I put my hand on his elbow. "Dad, Veronica has to go. She was just doing us a favor, you know?" I had to tread lightly, to get Veronica out of there before my dad could humiliate himself further, but without letting him on to the fact that I was trying to rush her away from him. It was a whole dance, and there was a fifty-fifty chance it would blow up in my face.

"Wait a minute," Dad said, an edge creeping into his voice.

Sixty-forty. Best case, I realized.

"I see what's happening," he snarled. He grabbed Veronica by the wrist. "Young lady, has my son made *advances* toward you?"

I glanced around, wishing like hell the ground would open up and swallow me whole.

"It's nothing like that, Mr. Mantle," Veronica said, extracting her hand and shooting me a nervous look. "This was strictly professional."

Dad huffed, spit flying from his mouth as he did. Veronica stepped back as delicately as she could. "I see," he said. "Of *course* a young lady such as yourself wouldn't date the likes of my son. You're powerful . . . aggressive . . . an overachiever." He shot me a withering look. "The exact opposite of Reginald here. The lioness needs an alpha at her side and alas, my son is *not* that."

My pulse hammered against my temples. "That's enough, Dad," I said, trying—again—to be casual about it, even though I was a heartbeat away from exploding with rage.

Ignoring me, my dad wrapped an arm around Veronica's waist and gave her a "playful" little pinch. "What do you say I take you out after this little event and show you a bit of that renowned Mantle . . . *hospitality*?"

"Dad," I begged, not caring anymore about possibly making him angry, "I'm warning you—please . . ."

"Mr. Mantle, I'm sorry to be so blunt, but this is beyond inappropriate," Veronica snapped, jerking herself away from my father. Her patience had finally worn thin. "I'm underage, and you're married."

"Minor details," my father said. "I know what girls like you want."

The pounding in my temples turned into a tsunami. Without thinking, I grabbed my father by his collar. "I SAID, THAT'S ENOUGH!"

"Reggie, don't!" Veronica cried.

"I think you've had a little too much Scotch," I whispered to my dad as vehemently as I could manage. "Why don't I call you an Uber and you can sleep it off?"

He wrenched himself free. "Get your hands off me, you insubordinate little brat!"

He raised one hand high, winding up to really—well, I knew what he was planning to do.

I closed my eyes and braced myself for the blow, but it never came.

"Mr. Mantle, please," Veronica said calmly, "Do you really want to do this? Here? Now?" She tilted her head toward the small crowd of guests who were cautiously peering our way.

Dad stared at us, breathing hard. "Fine," he said grudgingly. "I have investors to deal with, anyway." He sneered as he straightened, smoothing out his clothes and his hair. "But a bit of friendly advice to you—don't waste your time on this one." He jerked a thumb angrily in my direction. "He's . . . mediocre. A pretender."

He gave me one last glance, then stuffed his hands into his pockets. Turning to walk away from this whole mess, my father offered one final parting shot.

"In the end, he'll only disappoint you. That's all he's ever done for me."

∧∧∧

Ronnie made a point of not bringing that day up with me again—she knew the last thing I wanted was her concern or pity. But she'd seen me at one of my lowest points, and it wasn't something I could just forget about.

Even though I sure did try.

Whatever. Back in the moment, I shook my head and did my best to shake those thoughts out of my mind. So my family life wasn't perfect—so what? Whose was?

Okay, maybe Archie's dad wouldn't have ever lashed out at his kid the way mine does . . . but Archie's dad *died*. He was helping a person who'd been stranded on the side of the road, and he got hit by a freaking car. I mean, talk about nice guys finishing last. So I didn't have a nice guy for a father. At least . . . At least I still had one?

My dad wasn't perfect. Far from it. But that didn't mean I had to go all emo-boy over it like Jones over here. I mean, the day I had anything more in common with that guy than a zip code, was the day I just said screw it all and tossed myself into the Sweetwater.

In other words: *never gonna happen.*

But for now, Jughead was glued to his phone, obsessively stalking his little sister and dealing with whatever drama was going on with that new-and-improved, one-big-happy-family gang that he was supposedly "king" of. And Archie was doing his very Archiest best, setting things up with a grim, determined set to his jaw. Which meant that neither of them was focused on me.

And that? Was perfect.

Because I had plans of my own for this poker night. And in order to make sure my plans went off without a hitch, I had a few odds and ends to take care of. Quickly and quietly, under the radar . . .

Just like your boy Reggie does best.

So you want to know my story? I warn you—it's not a pretty one.

Well, if you're certain you want to hear it, then. I will offer this:

Mine is the grimmest of fairy tales. Narrated by a cipher—a wounded outcast, abandoned and alone—and hinging on a harrowing legacy.

Legacy, you ask? What legacy?

You burn with curiosity: the sordid details of human cruelty—that casual, crippling cruelty that is so particular, so essential, to the very soul of a young girl.

What legacy? *I laugh. Why, my own, of course. Who else's could it possibly be?*

However tragic, however sordid, it is mine to bear alone. And so, I do. I embrace it.

I was targeted, I was tormented, until my only choice was to vanish into thin air itself.

But I've made good use of my time as an imaginary creature, as this nonentity hovering on the peripheries of others' awareness and experiences.

I bided my time—after my . . . accident. I was patient, but inside I was roiling with thick, potent anger. Waiting for my moment. Waiting for the exact right time to enact my plot.

And now it's finally here. The moment is upon me.

The forest is still, yet alive: a paradox of quiet, constant movement.

They're here. *The girls.*

A crackle, a tentative foot on an unsteady path. An echo of brash voices and false bravado running a tinny undercurrent beneath the chatter. Nerves lighting the air like tiny pinpricks of electricity. Bottle rockets, a slash of lightning, the flicker of an open flame: These minuscule moments of combustion erupting, threatening to tear a hole in the very fabric of the night.

Heavier steps now. Breathless movement, momentum. My skin thrills with realization, with anticipation.

They're here, the maidens. Because I have summoned them. They creep through the woods unaware—unafraid of me and unafraid of that which lies just beyond the edges of their vision, of their consciousness. They don't see me; they don't sense me. They don't understand my power. They don't know that they are here at all because it is my will alone.

How silly of them. How small-minded, shortsighted.

Girls can be such foolish creatures.

I should know. After all, wasn't I the original jester? The most foolheartedly hopeless of them all? It's why I was so brutally targeted.

But I will remind them: I am more than that memory. This is my purpose, the reason I have come to this place. Here. Today. Now.

I will remind them. Of all the myriad dangers that lurk in the dark. In the woods. In our hearts. In the blood of their fellow young women.

I will remind them that the most monstrous beast known to man is ourselves.

Myself.

I will remind them. And they will see me.

They will see.

CHAPTER NINE

BETTY

Be careful what you wish for. That's how the saying goes, right? I should've kept that in mind.

I should've *clung* to it, back when we were still on the bus, still mostly dry and semisafe (or at least, so it seemed). Back before Cheryl had insisted on traipsing off into the woods down some random nonpath, some route that *I* swore to her was visible on Toni's phone.

(On the phone it *was* visible. Less so now that we were pushing through the storm toward . . . who even knew what.)

I should have refused to lead this charge.

Too late now.

I was an Adventure Scout; I can do this. I can always do it. Of course, that's what I said. I didn't hesitate, not for a minute.

What's *wrong* with me?

No, really—that's not rhetorical. What *is* it about me that leads me to do these things?

Why do I always charge ahead no matter the circumstance, assuming that I absolutely know the way? That I can absolutely handle myself in any—and every—situation?

I mean, hasn't history taught me *anything* yet?

Because there *is* something wrong with me. My mom, my friends . . . they may try to reassure me, they may do their best to comfort me and to tell me I'm normal, I'm good. But that can't be entirely true. There's no way.

Think about all that stuff Polly was feeding me about me having "the serial killer gene" when she was trying to brainwash me with her cult propaganda. There's a reason she went straight to *that* story, used *that* hyperspecific, horrifying line on me. It didn't even have to be true. Because the *real* truth, the plain truth, was enough of a horror show.

The skeletons in my personal closet don't need any embellishment.

Because among all the other things I, Betty Cooper, might be?

I'm also the daughter of the Black Hood.

Serial killer gene or not (the jury was still out on whether Polly had been trying to gaslight me or not), that truth runs blood deep, down to the very fiber of my DNA.

Betty Cooper has a dark side. Always has, always will.

And the thought that keeps me up at night, staring, unblinking, at the ceiling, as my heart races in my throat?

What if the darkness is the real me?

The snap of a twig underfoot roused me out of my little pity-party reverie. I ducked just in time to avoid being clotheslined by a low-hanging branch. *Get it together, Betty.* If we were going to make it to Sweetwater Pines in one piece, this was no time to spiral.

"Ugh, a mosquito the size of a pterodactyl just literally *attacked* me." It was Ginger. On cue, my shoulders tightened at the sound of her shrill voice. A reminder of how many people were out here, with me, relying on me.

I didn't *want* to lose my patience, my temper . . . possibly my mind. Not in the woods, in the storm, with all these girls counting on me. But damn if their whining and second-guessing wasn't slowly but surely getting under my skin.

"A watched pot never boils," Veronica said smoothly, before I had a chance to snap or say something I might regret. Sometimes it's like she's actually inside my head. But I hoped she wasn't reading my mind right now; it wasn't pretty.

Veronica gave a reassuring smile to Ginger. "Or whatever the survivalist equivalent of that saying would be. Obviously, Betty's doing her best. We'll be there as soon as possible. Remember: We want to get there in one piece, too. Which means being careful."

"Sure, yeah. Careful. But seriously? This place is *swarming* with bugs," Ginger went on, undaunted by Veronica's entreaties. Girl was the reason the phrase *vocal fry* had been invented in the first place. Her voice was setting my teeth on edge.

I looked at the phone in my hand. One bar left, and just barely at that. The map spread across the screen, the live view of the forest unfurling in a sea of green that taunted me with a vision of sunny, idyllic summer days here. Nothing like the muddy sludge we were currently slogging through. As if to punctuate my thought, my foot went down in an extra-deep patch of muddy slime. *Of course.* I wiggled it loose without too much trouble, a loud squelching sound punctuating my foot's freedom, and then grimaced when I realized exactly how much mud had run down the heel of my shoe.

Perfect. Muddy, waterlogged shoes were exactly the cherry on this hell-hike sundae.

I stopped, turning to face the girls. They looked like extras from a war movie: grime-streaked, exhausted. But for the most part, they were trying to keep their brave faces on (Ginger not-withstanding). Looking at their strained expressions, I softened.

"It's not too far now," I said, trying to keep the weariness out of my own voice. "Maybe a quarter of a mile. But, it *is* uphill, so. Fair warning."

I watched as their faces registered that information. Uphill, yeah. This hell hike was only going to get more intense. Not to mention, it was still raining, and the woods grew thicker with each step forward we took. We'd come to the end of the paved road about an hour ago, and in the woods, the walk was much slower going.

The forest canopy protected us from the worst of the

downpour, which was a blessing, but the terrain was way more challenging than the road had been, obviously. And let's just say it was quickly becoming clear that I was maybe the *only* Vixen who'd ever been an Adventure Scout in her previous life.

"Uphill, we got it," Toni said. She brushed a soggy lock of pink hair out of her face and back from her forehead. "Not a problem. We can do this." Now she looked at the others, her expression even more challenging than mine. "Right?"

Heads bobbed in lukewarm assessment. Clearly no one felt inspired to agree with total abandon. I didn't blame them. But I *also* knew that, at this point, we had absolutely no other choice. It was way too late to try to make our way back to the bus (both figuratively and literally—the sun, already limited because of the storm, had nearly disappeared, and walking toward the road in this weather, in the dark? That was basically a death wish. I might have had a darkness hiding inside me, but my inner Adventure Scout wasn't going to knowingly put these girls in harm's way. I definitely wasn't that far gone yet).

I cast a pleading look at Cheryl. *Rally the troops.* She got it.

"Vixens!" she said, brisk. "The night draws nearer and I, for one, would prefer to greet it from the comfort of our own cabin at Sweetwater Pines. So I suggest you *all*"—she shot a glare at Ginger, who flinched—"dig deep and get it together. Otherwise, I just might be forced to reevaluate your fitness to serve on our squad. And we wouldn't want *that*, now, would we?" She arched a challenging eyebrow, leaving the question dangling in the air, ominous.

A few girls grumbled, but one by one, we all began to move again—carefully, with deliberate paces. I stuffed Toni's phone into my pocket for safekeeping—it wasn't going to stay dry there, exactly, but at least it probably wouldn't get any wetter than it already was.

"Not quite the bonding experience we were hoping for, huh?" Veronica slipped into step next to me. "I'm all for a cheer retreat, and maybe I'm not still the *total* rich-girl diva I was when I first showed up in Riverdale, but how about next time we keep our retreating simple—and *way* more luxe? I'm thinking the BodyHoliday wellness retreat in Saint Lucia. They *swim* refills of coconut water out to your personal ocean float when you get thirsty." She closed her eyes for a moment, caught up in the memory of island wellness retreats past.

"That sounds . . . decadent," I said, laughing. "Although right now, the last thing I want to think about is more water."

"Fair enough," Veronica said. "I'm just putting the option out there."

"Ginger aside," I said, "how do you think the girls are holding up? It's been a day." I spoke tentatively; I wasn't sure I wanted to know the answer. And Veronica would never be anything less than straight with me.

I braced myself for a dose of brutal honesty when she took a breath, obviously gathering her thoughts before answering.

"Hanging on," she offered, cautious. "I don't think any of them are going to be writing any effusive Yelp reviews when this is all over. But no one was hurt in the mini accident, we're all alive and in one piece, and theoretically not too far from camp."

"You're right, we're not." That much I could offer with confidence right now. "If nothing else, I can promise you that we're on the right track and we're close."

"Well, there you go," she said, happy. "This trip may have gotten off to a rocky—or, rather, a *rainy* start—but soon enough we'll be at the camp, changed into dry, cozy clothes, and roasting marshmallows. If not over an actual campfire outdoors, then we'll find an accessible burner in the kitchen. We are nothing if not strong, resourceful women, after all."

"That does sound dreamy." I'd been fantasizing about my Bulldogs fleece pants since Cheryl first mentioned cashmere back on the bus.

Mostly, I just wanted to be indoors, out of the woods. It was a cliché, of course—fairy-tale stuff, being afraid of the woods in some dark, vague, ill-defined way. But deep, dark, scary woods weren't just the stuff of legends—in Riverdale, they were the site of some truly indelible traumas.

"I will say this," Veronica started, breaking into my thoughts. "As unpleasant as this little impromptu nature walk is? It still beats the last time you and I were traipsing through the woods together."

The girl *could* read my mind. No wonder we were ride-or-die.

"Penelope Blossom's sick hunt." I remembered all too well. Some nights, that fateful evening unfolded on instant replay, a mini movie in my brain that couldn't—wouldn't—be erased.

"Archie fighting that man-bear. Jughead facing off against Chic." Veronica's eyes were dark, recalling.

"Us playing Russian roulette with Penelope's poison." I swallowed, sure I could taste the thick, viscous liquid in my throat all over again.

"We survived that," Veronica said, bright. "This? In comparison? Is a cakewalk. A Milk Bar funfetti cake, which—this is my solemn vow to you, Betty Cooper—I will have hand-delivered from the city the second we step foot back in Riverdale again."

"Deal." I forced a grin for her sake. But thinking about that night, replaying the images—bramble and branches and twigs, thorns, roots, all of it twisting and winding and reaching for us like claws—all I could see was my father. The Black Hood. Stripped of his mask, his face stark against the moonlight of another ink-dark night. Pale, as the blood seeped from the wound on his arm.

The wound *I'd* inflicted. The gunshot *I'd* fired.

Penelope had pitted me against my most bitter secret, my darkest half, and asked me to confront it: to destroy it lest it destroy me first. "*Don't make me do this,*" I'd said, but my father . . . he raised his own gun; he aimed it at me.

He was *prepared* to destroy me. He didn't hesitate, not for a second.

Well, I wasn't prepared to destroy him. I'd never wanted that. But like always, I did what had to be done.

I fired, yes. But I'd shot him in the arm. I won the round, but I let him live. I'd beaten Penelope's game.

That's what I'd thought then, anyway.

Until she shot him point-blank, bullet to the brain.

That moment . . . My father was evil. Unquestionably, he deserved to die. But he was still *my father.* Did I deserve to lose him? To *watch* as he was robbed of his life?

I'd tried to avoid the woods after that, understandably.

But here I was again, somehow. Against my own better judgment. Back in the woods. In the storm. In the dark.

The stakes still high, others needing me. I wasn't alone now.

A branch crackled, off to one side, and I whirled.

What was that?

I *wasn't* alone, of course—the Vixens were here, cautiously stepping into the footprints Veronica and I left in our wake as we slowly advanced through the woods.

But it wasn't *their* footsteps that I'd just heard.

A flash, a blur—a figure, amorphous and gauzy in a muted, glowing white haze—darted past.

I screamed.

I couldn't help it. Reflexively, I stumbled, staggering back, scrabbling against a tree truck and struggling to regain my footing.

"What is it?" Veronica was at my side in a second, Toni and Cheryl close behind. The rest of the Vixens chirped anxiously, scanning the woods to see what had set me off.

I blinked, trying to steady the fuzzy, wavering lines of the forest that danced in my vision. "I . . . don't know," I said, honest. All I saw around me, in any direction, were trees and rain and fearful Vixens. *If* something had run out from the brush, dashed across my path in pursuit of . . . something beyond my scope of vision . . .

Well, *if* that had happened, there was no trace of it left behind now.

I felt jittery, the way I used to when my mother would force Adderall down my throat in some misguided, desperate attempt to keep me acting "normal." The sick joke was, in the end, it only made things weirder—made me feel like my skin was too tight, my thoughts too fragmented. It made me doubt myself . . . Just like I was doing now.

"I thought—" I stopped, looked at the gathered Vixens again. Whatever *it* was that I thought I had seen, it wasn't there now, and they hadn't seen a glimpse of it. So, what was the point, then, in saying anything? At best I'd look insane, and at worst, I'd freak everyone out.

There's nothing out here, Betty, I told myself. I blinked again, scanned the area again. *Nothing.* And the sooner I got the Vixens to the camp, the sooner I'd be safe, sheltered from the woods and all its lurking dangers and barbed, violent memories. The sooner we'd *all* be safe.

"Never mind," I said, hitching my backpack higher on my shoulders and standing up straight. "Look." I pointed at the sky, at the mild, probably temporary, clearing in the rain. "We're almost there.

"Let's go."

CHAPTER TEN

CHERYL

"Wonder of wonders, Vixens. Could this actually be what I think it is, and not merely a mirage? Could we actually have arrived at our bargain basement Valhalla at last?"

"It's not a figment of your imagination, Cheryl. Or, if it is, then this is one impressive collective hallucination. But if so, I don't even care. Camp Sweetwater Pines, I daresay you are a sight for sore eyes!" Veronica rushed past me, grabbing Betty's hand and dragging her through the wooden archway proclaiming the entrance to the campgrounds, kicking up mud in their wake as they ran. Ahead of us lay waterlogged fields of grass pocketed with enormous, murky puddles. In the distance, a set of cabins were arranged in a rickety horseshoe. Never had anything so resoundingly rustic looked so appealing.

"Tsk–tsk," I said, turning to Toni. "So dramatic, those two."

Toni grinned. "Maybe. But after that trek, you have to admit that Sweetwater Pines is definitely looking *sweet*."

"Indeed, *ma chérie*. Thus far, this place is nothing less than our own personal Shangri-la," I said, agreeing. "And praise the radiant Goddess above that we've all made it here in one piece, relatively unscathed."

"Well, don't speak *too* soon—Ginger's still moaning about her bug bites," Toni said. She rolled her eyes.

"Emotional fortitude is not that girl's strong suit," I replied. "But as long as she's not moaning to *me* right now, I'm pleased as punch to be here. Let's get to our cabin and get dry. I can just feel the cashmere tracksuit against my silky-smooth skin as we speak."

"Maybe don't unpack those bags just yet." It was Veronica, cutting in with more authority than the situation actually warranted.

"You had another plan, pray tell?" I flashed my most challenging glare at her.

"Calm down, Cheryl." She sighed. "I just meant, we should probably check in at the front office? Like, see if Coach Grappler's friends left us any kind of orientation guide, or a map or something?"

"*Le sigh*. How drearily responsible of you," I said, airy and bored. "But now that we're here, I, for one, am ready to seek shelter from the elements, regardless of the dubious 'rustic' appeal of this place." Beyond the archways and the drenched field, the cluster of ramshackle cabins beckoned. Small lanterns hung above their doorways, though none were illuminated just then. "These must be the bunks, *mais oui*? Let's go claim ours and make ourselves comfortable."

"But how do we know which one is ours?" Toni asked. "Or does it not matter, if we're the only ones here?"

"Exactly why I think we need to hit the main office. Look." Veronica pointed. "That must be it. I'm betting there's more information there, or keys to the cabins, at least." She paused. "Honestly, given that the camp isn't even open right now, my confidence may well be misplaced."

She had gestured toward a smaller structure—more of a shack, really. It had a rusted screen door that swung and clattered against its frame in the wind, and a battered old sign that read WELCOME. Frankly, it looked the very opposite of welcoming.

"Well, it's either the main office or an elaborate ruse leading to a trap designed solely for us," I said, thinking: *even odds*.

"Hey—it wouldn't be the first time," Toni said. "But I actually think we're safe right now—for once."

I looked at her, arching a perfectly shaped eyebrow. "Well, *ma petite fleur*, that was a jinx if I ever heard one," I said, wry. "But *allons-y*." I grabbed her hand and, together, we led the way.

⋀⋀⋀

Up close, the euphemistically termed "Welcome Office" was drearier than it had appeared from beneath the entry archway. I personally wouldn't have thought it possible, and yet.

Strangely, though, for how abandoned and empty it seemed,

it also didn't feel like we were the first people to cross its mold-infested threshold that day; a trail of soggy footprints crisscrossed the floor as we stepped cautiously inside.

"Hello?" Toni called as we moved into the space. "Guys," she said, turning back to us, "there's no one in here." A wave of must and mildew gusted toward us as she did.

"Okay, well, we didn't really think there *would* be anyone here," Betty said, sounding skeptical. "Right? Coach Grappler pulled strings to get us in, but the place isn't *technically* open."

"True enough, dear cousin," I replied. "But nonetheless"— I gestured, wrinkling my nose against the fusty scent—"*these* footprints suggest that we do, in fact, have company. Somewhere on-site, if not right here, right now." It wasn't an appealing thought. The last thing I needed was a retreat weekend spent rubbing elbows with the proletariat.

"Maybe maintenance crew? The owners must have sent someone to open this place up, right?" Betty said.

"That's certainly the most positive spin one could give it. I'll take it. I do so love that Pollyanna spirit, Betts! Hey—what's that?" Just to the left, clinging limply to a dented file cabinet, a Post-it note was waving our way. "Pardon," I said to Toni, giving her shoulder a squeeze as I sashayed past to have a closer look.

"Is it for us?" Veronica asked, craning her neck with curiosity.

"Maybe," I said, plucking it—and a nasty thicket of

spiderwebs—from the file cabinet. "'For all cheer squads checking into Sweetwater Pines fall cheer retreat, please report to the rec hall down the path.'" I looked up. "Well, I guess you were right about someone opening this place up for us. Good to know we're not totally left to our own devices out here in the wilds, in any case."

I turned to Ginger. "I sincerely hope you've found your bug spray," I said. "Because it looks like we're not done trekking just yet."

"Wait," Betty said, a spark lighting up her eyes. "*All* cheer squads. So then . . ."

She trailed off, perturbed.

Veronica made a face. "I see where you're going with this, B. So then we're *definitely* sharing this camp with someone."

"Yes, and with the way the note is worded, I have to wonder," Betty said, calm and logical, "exactly how *many* other squads are here with us for the weekend?"

What? My eyes narrowed. *Other squads?*

"Oh, *hell* no," I said. "Over my dead—and immaculately preserved—body are we sharing this space with rando farm team–level cheer squads for the weekend." Not a threat, a promise.

"To the rec hall, minions," I said, game face ready. "Let's get to the bottom of this mysterious screed."

⌒⌒⌒

After yet another soggy trudge yonder and down the way, we came upon a desolate-looking structure that vaguely resembled a barn. Somewhat surprisingly, the camp was divided by relatively clear, wide paths that surely were actual dirt rather than the quicksand-esque rivers of mud we'd had to traverse just to find this infernal building in the first place. Behind me, the Vixen vassals had dissolved into a tedious flurry of inane chatter that was nearly driving me to delirium.

"OMG, you guys, I'm telling you, I'm just now realizing that a friend of my friend went to Sweetwater Pines, like a million years ago. Seriously." It was Brigitte Reilly, a sophomore and a newer addition to the squad. "I can't believe I, like, just figured it out."

I could certainly believe it. Beside me, Toni gave me a playful elbow to the ribs, knowing exactly what I was thinking. Brigitte had stamina in spades, and her pear-shaped musculature made for the perfect base for all our pyramid stunts, but to call her a simpleton would have been overstating it. Even for a drama queen like *moi*.

Unfortunately, whatever wretched fable she was regurgitating to the rest of the squad, she'd somehow managed to pique their curiosity. Most of my Vixens were agape, hanging on her every word.

She giggled now, insipid. "Swear to god, there are, like, *so* many urban legends about this place."

"Like what?" Nancy Woods, sometime paramour of Chuck

Clayton and one of our star fliers, was utterly breathless to hear more.

"Literally, *so* many. Like, I heard from my friend who went here that a kid *drowned* in the lake one summer while the lifeguards on duty were making out. They were, like, so busy climbing all over each other they never even saw it happen. And then—his *mother* went insane, can you even believe it? And she came back next summer and, like, stalked all the counselors who'd come back. She straight-up murdered them *all*."

Betty shot Brigitte some formidable side eye. "Uh, actually, that's the plot of the first *Friday the Thirteenth* movie."

"Huh." If Brigitte was surprised, she was nevertheless totally undaunted by this revelation. She dropped her voice, as though there were anyone around to overhear this ludicrous conversation but us. "Well, okay, so maybe you're right."

"I am," Betty assured her. "Also, anything you might have heard about a scary, burned-up school janitor with knives for fingers who stalks teenagers in their sleep? Also false."

Brigitte rolled her eyes. "Um, hello—everyone knows about Freddy Krueger! Don't be ridic, Betty." She giggled. "But, okay, I did hear—and this one is for sure totally true—that there was a girl here a few summers ago, a camper. And she was, like, really badly hazed. Bullied, I mean."

I rolled my eyes. "We know what *hazed* means."

"No, you don't get it—I mean, she *died* here. At the camp. Like she was hazed to the point of getting *literally* killed."

Accordingly, all the Vixens gathered around her shivered, in unison.

"Unlikely," I snapped. "It's the kind of story that could be easily verified with a quick Google search." I whipped out my phone and glanced at the screen. "Which I will perform just as soon as I'm getting more than one paltry bar of service in this godforsaken land that Wi-Fi forgot."

"Babe," Toni said, slipping a hand into my own. "Let's just go inside and see what—or *who*—we're dealing with."

"As always, dear TeeTee, your advice is on point. And, if I recall correctly, it was Betty herself who said that hope springs eternal."

Betty looked at me. "Actually, Cheryl? *You* were the one who said that."

I considered this. "Hmm. Well, as you all are all too aware, *my* advice is always on point, too. Vixens: Let's go inside."

I led the way.

∿∿∿

The barn—or, excuse me, the *rec hall*—doors groaned as I pushed them open, the damp, fetid air irritating my delicate lungs and making me cough. I can't say exactly what I was expecting to find (other than maybe a few stray extras from a second-tier summer-stock performance of *Deliverance*). But I will for damn certain tell you that I was absolutely *not* expecting nigh twentysomething lissome young creatures in various and sundry high school cheer regulation tracksuits. Approximately half of them were in gray and green, a large *S* above the left breast of their warm-up jackets, and the other half were in red and gold . . . In other words, the school colors of . . .

"The Baxter High *Ravenettes*?" I shrieked. What on earth were *they* doing here on our weekend? Other than sniffing around to steal *our* prime routines, of course.

The tallest of the Ravenettes, dark hair wound high on her head in a double row of braid crowns, stepped forward. I recognized her as the captain of the squad but wouldn't dare give her the satisfaction of registering the recognition.

"In the flesh," she practically purred, her voice silky. "What's it to you?" She looked extremely pleased with herself. "Come to see how you stack up against the best of the best? Spoiler alert? You don't."

I cleared my throat. "If you must know, you *charlatan*, what it *is* to me is that I was given to believe that we River Vixens had the run of this backwater campus for the weekend. Believe me, if I'd known we were expected to share the space, I would have canceled our reservation *tout suite*."

"What can I say?" the Ravenettes' captain asked, still grinning coyly. She glanced at her teammates, who flanked her in a formidable cluster. "You were obviously sorely misled, and I'm sorry for that. But *we've* been coming to

Sweetwater Pines for *our* cheer retreat on the third Saturday of every September since . . . well, since the Baxter High Ravenettes first took all-state in cheer stunt competition. They use ViewTube footage of our basket tosses to this day in cheer tutorials, you know." She gave me another small, smug smile—and, adding insult to injury, a slow, languid wink. "I'm Lizzie. And this year, we literally got an engraved invitation to come here."

She held out a small square of cardstock, but I waved it aside. "Not interested."

"Now, now, Cheryl," Veronica said, stepping forward and placing a hand on my shoulder. "While it may be true that, thus far, very little about this weekend has transpired quite as we expected, we're here now, and we may as well make the best of it. *All* of us, that is. I'm sure Coach Grappler will help clear up any misunderstandings as soon as she gets here. In the meantime, how about playing nice with our unexpected bunkmates?" She held out a hand. "I'm Veronica. Lodge. Riverdale High River Vixen."

"You should listen to your friend," said the presumed leader of the forest green and gray team, shaking Veronica's hand. "I'm Stasia, by the way. Short for Anastasia. I'm the captain of the Stonewall Prep Queens."

"Wait . . . *Stonewall*? You said Stonewall Prep?" Betty cut in. "So, you're in school with . . . I mean, my boyfriend goes to your school. Now he does. He's new—Jughead Jones."

"Jughead, yeah!" Stasia said, grinning. She looked at Betty, appraising. "So, *you're* the famous Betty Cooper?"

"I mean . . . I don't know about famous . . ." Betty trailed off. I couldn't tell how she felt about Stasia having heard of her, though, of course, it meant that her odious misanthrope boyfriend at least talked about her at his new school, which couldn't be a bad thing.

Stasia rolled her eyes. "I can't even tell you how many girls are crushing on him. He could totally have his pick. But I guess you've got him wrapped around your finger. For now, at least."

Ouch. Point to Stasia, she knew how to shoot to kill. At least fifteen different expressions flitted across Betty's face. I stepped in to save the poor girl. "Funny, that," I said. "I suppose when you're trapped, tucked away in those gothic turrets with nothing but your own incestuous company for entertainment, people's standards deteriorate quickly."

Betty shot me a look. "Thanks, Cheryl."

"So both of your teams are here for the weekend?" Veronica asked, still playing at gracious hostess and hastily trying to move past the awkwardness of the Jughead-related exchange. "Where are your coaches?"

"Um, *coaches*?" Lizzie stifled a snort. "No, dear, we don't have a babysitter. Since we were specifically invited, our coach assumed there'd be some kind of supervision here for us when we showed up." She grinned. "Oh well. What they don't know won't hurt them."

"Maybe whoever is in charge is still on the way?" Betty offered. "They could have been caught up in the storm."

"Maybe," Lizzie echoed, mocking the high pitch of Betty's voice. She stepped closer to me, lowering her voice. "But here's the thing: Sweetwater Pines is the *Ravenettes'* playground." She tilted her head and gave me a smug grin. "*Maybe* we'll let you stick around, if you promise you can play nice."

"Hold up," Toni interjected. "We don't need to go all female *Lord of the Flies* on each other. The Vixens are just looking to get squared away in our cabin. We've been dreaming about four walls since our bus first ran off the road."

Lizzie nodded. "The cabin assignments were posted in the main office when the Queens got here. So they brought them down here themselves."

Stasia made a face. "We've been sharing so nicely." She held up a folded square of paper. "Read it and weep."

I snatched the note from her hand and unfolded it greedily. Quickly, I scanned the document. It had been typed and presumably computer-printed, but there were a few cross-outs in aggressive scrawls on the document. "*You* guys get cabin one, I see," I said to Stasia, suspicious. Generally speaking, number one of *anything* was reserved for me.

She sighed heavily. "The numbers have to do with where the cabins are on the field. It's not a rank or score."

"So you say. But I can't help but notice that we Vixens aren't assigned a cabin at all?" Well, that simply wouldn't do. I glared at Stasia.

"We were *literally* invited to this retreat," Stasia said. "Hence: assignments."

"It does make sense," Betty put in. "Coach Grappler said she got us in here as a favor. Maybe whoever made those assignments for the other squads never got the memo about us?" She shrugged.

"This is not exactly a deep-state conspiracy," Lizzie said, annoyed. "If you're going to be so extra about it, just take cabin two. Cabin three is less drafty, anyway."

"Understand: I will *always* be 'so extra about it,'" I said, looping an arm through Toni's. But the subject had grown beyond wearisome. All I really wanted at this point was a mattress to lay my head on—no matter how threadbare or—*ugh*—mildewed.

I beckoned to my girls. "Let's go set up in our bunk, Vixens. *Cabin two*, and I think we can consider this matter settled."

The Ravenettes and the Queens watched, silent, as we stalked off.

CHAPTER ELEVEN

☀ RIVW WEATHER   1 min. ago

Sit tight, Riverdale residents! We know that brief lull in the storm was a welcome respite, but we're sorry to tell you that no one is out of the woods just yet. Our satellites tell us that within the hour we'll be seeing another storm surge as well as another round of high winds, with gusts at 30–40 mph. Expect downed trees and possibly extensive property damage. Don't be caught unprepared in the case of a power outage, and keep off the roads. Stay tuned to RIVW for all your storm updates throughout the weekend. We care about your safety!

—RIVW.com and affiliates

∿∿∿

JUGHEAD

If there was a storm raging outside, you wouldn't know it downstairs at La Bonne Nuit, in the belly of the game-night beast. Even with the bluster outside, it felt like half the teen population in Riverdale had turned out for our "little" poker night: Kevin Keller was cuddled up with Frankie Valdez at a side table watching all the action go down; Sweet Pea and

Fangs were faced off against Peaches 'N Cream and some other Serpents and Poisons at a table of their own; and Archie, Munroe, Reggie, and I were seated at the primary poker table, smack in the center of the room, deep into the third round of the evening so far. Perched at the bar, Chuck Clayton sipped a beer and called out the occasional semi-playful heckle with just the appropriate amount of plausible deniability.

"Watch that one, yo," he shouted, tipping his bottle at Reggie. "He's counting cards, for sure."

Reggie smirked over his cards, fanned out in his hand, but he didn't dignify the comment with a response. That boy was laser-focused on his game.

"A little less commentary from the peanut gallery, please," Munroe called. "Some of us are trying to concentrate."

Personally, I thought Chuck was only half kidding. With the storm raging outside, the only thunder in here came in the form of earth-shattering applause every time Reggie won another hand. Which was happening often. Like, maybe *suspiciously* often? I liked Reggie—or rather, I liked him well enough, despite the fact that he used to pummel me on the regular sophomore year when Archie and I were briefly on the outs, strictly for the crime of being nonconformist by nature. I liked him, I guessed—but that didn't mean I totally trusted him.

Still, it felt too early in the evening to go on some kind of vigilante rampage calling him out for . . . what, getting lucky a few too many times in a row? What was I, the poker police now?

I had better things to do. Like try to win a few hands of my own before the night was over. I glanced at Reggie's impressive pile of chips. "Mantle, how did we not know you were Vegas-pro level?"

"What can I say, Jones? Everyone's got their secrets. I like to keep you guys guessing." He peered at his hand again, and then at the sizable pile of cash in the middle of the table. "Call." He meant Munroe, who promptly revealed his hand . . . and the (admittedly, pitiful) bluff he'd been trying to pull off.

"Crap." Munroe slammed his cards down on the table and shoved more bills into the pot. Archie and I quickly folded and followed suit.

"Well, *whatever* your secret is, you sure are on a winning streak tonight," Archie said. He took a swig from the cut-crystal tumbler to his right, clearly savoring the aged bourbon Veronica had insisted we crack open for the occasion.

My ears pricked up at that. It was an innocent-enough comment, but I knew my friend well enough to pick up on the subtle barb behind the statement. And I knew where he was coming from, too.

"Jealous, Andrews? Not a good look on you," Reggie said, leering. He swiped up everyone's folded hands and started to shuffle for a new round. "I may not be all up on fashion like our girl Veronica, but even I could tell you, green with envy clashes with that carrottop."

Archie bristled, clearly reacting to Reggie's use of "our" girl when he mentioned Veronica. General consensus was that Varchie was "endgame," but she did have an interlude with Reggie while Archie was away last year. And, personally, I didn't have the sense that Reggie was totally over it.

I didn't think Archie did, either. Especially not from the way a tiny vein in his forehead was twitching right now.

"In your dreams, bro," Archie said. Was it my imagination, or was he straining to sound casual? There went that forehead vein again.

Suddenly, the sharp, staccato sound of a duck quacking broke through the tension of the moment.

"Whose phone is that?" Sweet Pea snapped. "I thought we were all trying to concentrate."

"Not a phone," Reggie said. He held up the BuyPad he'd been using for security. "A push notification. There's someone upstairs." He jabbed at the screen, unlocking the door for our surprise guest. "There."

We all turned to see who would come down the stairs. "And here I thought everyone we knew was actually already down here," I said.

"Not *everyone*."

I recognized that voice and jumped up. "JB?"

She stood at the top of the stairs alongside her friend Ricky.

They were both soaked from the storm, but their eyes glittered as they took in the scene.

"This is *so* cool," Ricky said, grinning with admiration.

"It is," I agreed, walking toward them. "It's also not exactly PG-13 down here." I glanced at JB. "What are you *doing* here?"

JB rolled her eyes. "Oh, please. If you didn't want us to crash, you shouldn't have been blabbing about the whole thing to Betty right in front of my face."

"I definitely *wasn't* blabbing 'right in front of your face,'" I countered. "And while I'm impressed at your surveillance skills, I need to reiterate—you can't stay here."

"Why not?"

"For one thing, Dad would kill me."

She gave me a withering look. "Only if you tell him."

"JB . . ." I didn't want to embarrass her by forcibly dragging her out of the speakeasy, but she seemed determined to let it come to that.

"Jug, I'm basically a Serpent. I don't know why you won't just accept that."

"Even if that *were* true—and it's not," I said, "you're *also* 'basically' underage."

Peaches 'N Cream stood up from her own game, cutting in to diffuse the awkwardness of the moment. "JB, there'll be other card games. Plenty. And you can sit right next to me at the Poisons' table when the time is right. I promise, I'll save you a seat."

JB narrowed her eyes at me. "You're not *really* kicking me out, are you, big brother?"

I shrugged. "You gonna make me say it?" I didn't relish this moment, that was for sure.

She gave another dramatic roll of her eyes and huffed loudly. "Seriously? You are so *lame*."

"You're certainly not the first person to tell me that," I said.

"Come on, Ricky. Forget this place." JB grabbed her lackey's hand roughly and stormed back up the stairs, feet thudding heavily as she stomped out.

As the door swung shut behind them, I looked at Peaches. "I didn't realize you and JB had such a connection." If I wasn't ready for my kid sister to be a Serpent, I *definitely* wasn't up for her being a Poison.

Peaches shrugged. "Kid's looking for a mentor. She's feeling a little . . . abandoned these days."

I bristled. "She has me."

Peaches cocked her head. "Like I say. A kid her age needs a reliable presence."

Ouch. The air crackled, thick with tacit implications and accusations. No one seemed to know quite how to react.

After a beat, though, Reggie jumped up. "All right." He slapped his palms on the table, like he was finally getting down to the real, *serious* business now. "Is this a poker game or a Sunday church service? Why so serious, guys?"

Munroe gave a low *whoop* at that, eager and approving. "Hells yeah, man. Back to the game!"

"Exactly. Except—what if we made things interesting?" Reggie grinned.

"What did you have in mind?" Archie asked, running his hand through his hair until it stood up in spikes, as alert and curious as the expression on his face.

"How about this: next round, double or nothing?"

The collective gasp in the room was like something from an old sitcom "audience" track it was so dramatic. Pretty much everyone in the room's jaw dropped a good inch or two—my own included. The other games were clearly over, everyone invested in what was going to go down at the high rollers' table. My jaw fell farther as I watched Reggie push all his winnings from the last hand back into the center of the table. Apparently, he was dead serious about this.

"Man, you're insane." Munroe whistled, in either admiration or disbelief (or both). "But, okay. I'm in." He pushed his own money into the center of the table. "Wait," he said, having another thought. He pulled a wallet out of his jeans pocket and fished a few extra twenties out. "Go big or go home, right? That's what we all came for."

"Sure is." Reggie began to shuffle, the cards arcing and fanning out beneath his fingers like a waterfall.

I looked at Archie. "Go big or go home," I echoed. It would

mean cleaning out the very last of the money I'd taken out specifically for this game—and it would probably also mean that this was going to be my last round of the night, and likely a painful one, at that. But, what the hell? Reggie was right: I couldn't compete with those rich kids from Stonewall, most of whom wouldn't have thought twice about doubling down during a friendly card game. But for one brief, foolish round, I could . . . pretend.

Stupid? Wasteful? Sure. But I was a high school kid. Foolish, spur-of-the-moment was my birthright. I decided to go with it, even if it was just this once.

There was a certain spirit of rebellion and total abandon in the air—blame it on the storm, or the size of the pot, or that weird chemical thing that happens when you shove a bunch of guys (and some tough-as-nails girls) into an underground speakeasy with drinks and money and games to play. Energy to burn, nowhere to put it. We were all keyed up, raring to go.

I tossed my buy-in into the pot. "I'm in."

"Me too," Archie said, following suit. Everyone in the room watching us cheered.

I heard the *click* of a BuyPhone camera before I saw the flash.

"Sorry," Kevin said as we blinked. "I just needed to capture this moment for posterity. Reggie Mantle doubling down is delightful *insanity*, and I am *here* for it. You guys don't care if I post this on Instagram, do you?"

"I mean, other than the illegal gambling and underage drinking, I can't see what about that would be a bad idea," I quipped. Not like everyone didn't know about the things that sometimes went on at La Bonne Nuit. Veronica for the most part managed to skate beneath the authorities' notice. But still.

"Point taken," Kevin admitted. "But I *will* be sending this pic to Veronica, because she's going to be totes thrilled with how well her poker night's gone off." He frowned at his phone. "Just as soon as the storm passes and we're getting service again, that is."

"I keep forgetting about the rain," I said. "After all that drama from RIVW and stuff, in the end, it almost feels like the storm barely affected us at all. Down here, anyway. I guess we got lucky, hiding out in the speakeasy."

Of course, I'd spoken too soon.

All at once, the overhead lights began to flicker.

"What's that?" I asked, sitting up, suspicious.

"Uh . . . three guesses . . ." Kevin said, looking nervous. All around the speakeasy, people started to rustle nervously in their seats.

That was when we heard it.

A *boom* so loud, so reverberant, it echoed even within our subterranean hideaway.

"Thunder," I said, stating the obvious, but that wasn't the right term for what we'd heard—a thunderclap that was mythical, nearly biblical in its force. "Thunder" felt inconsequential, ephemeral. This noise was apocalyptic, foreboding.

Suddenly, the flickering stopped. The speakeasy was bathed in darkness.

"Still feeling lucky?" Kevin asked, his voice shaking a little in the pitch black of the space between us.

CHAPTER TWELVE

BETTY

"I call bottom bunk!"

Cheryl stormed through the door to cabin two like a conquistador planting a flag. Behind her, the rest of the Vixens flooded into the cabin, pressing up against me and everyone jostling one another, vying to be the first in the room. The bunk had a faint smell of mildew, a thin layer of dust on every surface, and an elaborate network of cobwebs draping from the rafters, but at this exact moment in time, it was the coziest place I'd ever seen.

I held up my hands in a "calm down" gesture. "*Guys*. Just . . . be cool. We're here. We made it. The cabin's ours. This doesn't need to be, like, a vicious struggle."

"Speak for yourself, flunky," Cheryl retorted. "My advice to you all? Get while the getting is good. And I'm starting"—she surveyed the room, her hair a sheet of flame that whipped back and forth as she took in every detail of the space—"with *this* one!"

She marched triumphantly to the lone single bed pushed against the far wall. *Naturally*, I thought, groaning inwardly.

It was the only bed in the cabin that wasn't a bunk, which clearly suggested that it probably wasn't intended for any of us Vixens.

"Uh, Cheryl," I said, "I'm pretty sure that bed is meant for Coach Grappler."

She flashed me a grin. "Excellent. She can challenge me for it if and when she ever gets here."

Even Toni gave Cheryl a horrified look at that. "Cher, she's *going* to get here."

"Surely you're right, my love," Cheryl said, relenting. "But in the meantime, who better to carry the leadership torch?" She narrowed her eyes at the group. "Am I not squad captain?"

"Literally no one is questioning that," I said, sighing.

"Perfect. Then in that case, I can see no reason why anyone would question my choice to appropriate the leader's bed as my own." She dropped down onto the bed and kicked her legs up, pulling each rain boot off and crossing her legs at the ankles, lounging like a pinup queen. "It's a far cry from the pillow-top bedding we keep at Thistlehouse," she said, "but it will do nicely for now." She patted the space beside her. "TeeTee—a cuddle? Our journey was *so* arduous."

Toni smiled. "Just for a minute," she said, placing her own bag on the lower bed of the adjacent bunk to Cheryl's. "And I need to warn you—when spooning time is over? I'm going back to my bunk for actual sleep. These beds were *not* built for sharing."

"A valid point, but you *may* be underestimating my femi-nine wiles, *ma chérie*. I can be very persuasive when there's something that I want."

"Oh, Cheryl," Toni said, settling into the space beside her and closing her eyes, in an obvious moment of bliss, "you should know by now that I'd never, ever underestimate you."

Watching them, I felt more than a small pang of envy. Giving up a weekend with Jug meant even more of a sacrifice now that he was at Stonewall Prep. If he were here right now? I'd let him spoon as long as he wanted to, no matter how minuscule the beds were.

Veronica tapped me on the shoulder. "Girl, I know what you're thinking, because I'm right there with you."

"V," I sighed. "When did our relationships get so *complicated*?"

"Call it the Riverdale Effect," she said, giving me a squeeze. "But I, for one, have faith in true love."

"I wish I had your confidence," I said.

"Fake it till you make it?" she suggested. "And if nothing else, let us both be comforted by this harsh truth: These bunks are *definitely* not built for two."

"Stop complaining and start claiming your turf, Betty," Cheryl called. "There are exactly as many bunks as there are Vixens, so we're in a first-come, first-served situation. *Lean in*."

"I mean, there's the one left over that Coach Grappler is

going to have to take," I muttered. But there wasn't any bite to it; I didn't really care about the bunks. Not like the other girls who'd all taken on Cheryl's enthusiasm for claim-staking like this was some low-key rendition of The Hunger Games. In the three seconds it'd taken Veronica and me to wax nostalgic for our missing beaux, every bunk except one was taken.

Veronica moved to the remaining bunk, wrapping a palm around its metal frame. "It's not the Five Seasons, B. But it's ours." She glanced at the ceiling and shuddered. "Unless that gargantuan daddy longlegs decides to fight us for it in the dead of night. Because TBH, I'm guessing that thing would win."

"Step aside, V," I said, moving past her. "That spider's got nothing on me. I'll take the top bunk." Veronica Lodge feared very few things. But that didn't mean she *wanted* to get up close and personal with the insect population at Sweetwater Pines. I could easily take this one for the team.

"Don't be silly." She waved me off.

"Which of the two of us has actual experience camping?" I reminded her. "And therefore, more one-on-one experience with oversized bugs and creepy-crawlies?"

She smiled, relenting. "Thank you, and thank goodness," she said. "It's definitely off-brand for me to go all shrinking violet over something like a spider on steroids. And yet."

"And yet." I laughed, tossing my daypack up onto the bed and hoisting myself up after it. The springs creaked as I adjusted myself, inspecting the thin mattress and pancake-flat "pillow" the camp had provided. *Cushy.*

"How's the view up there?" Veronica asked. Her head popped over the edge of the bed, trying to check things out on tiptoe.

"I think I scared the spider off," I lied. "So, you know— we're already off to a good start."

"I know you're just saying that so I won't be afraid to go to bed tonight," Veronica replied. "And for that, I owe you a debt of gratitude."

Before I could respond, a crack split the air—so loud and forceful, the bedframes shook from the impact. "What the hell was that?" Ginger cried from one of the bottom bunks.

"Thunder," Toni said. "Did you see that crazy flash of lightning just now? The storm's kicking back up."

I propped myself onto an elbow. In the bed beside me, I saw Nancy Woods gingerly pulling back the scratchy wool blanket we'd all been given. She peered, curious, at the sheets, then shrank back, wrinkling her nose, and quickly yanked the wool blanket back in place.

She looked up and caught me watching her, then blushed.

"Hey," I said, "it beats that broken-down bus in the storm."

"True," she agreed, "but just *barely*, I think."

Another rumble of thunder broke out. Like a faucet had been turned on, buckets of rain suddenly lashed down, pounding insistently against the cabin roof.

"And, we've got at least one flood zone in here," Cheryl said, sitting up and pointing at a steady drip coming down in the corner of the bunk.

The air crackled as a bolt of lightning zigzagged across the sky. Suddenly, the lights in the cabin flickered off, then stuttered back on again.

"And a possible power outage," Toni put in. "The hits just keep on coming."

"Well," Cheryl said, "as long as we *do* still have electricity, might I suggest that some industrious young Vixen take it upon herself to procure for us a bucket for that leak?"

"Cheryl, you can't seriously be asking someone to volunteer to go out in that storm?" Veronica asked. "That's ludicrous. The *bucket* can wait until this dies down, at least a little. Not to mention, a real leader doesn't ask their followers to do anything they themselves aren't willing to do."

"And if I wanted a civics lesson, Veronica, you'd be the first person I'd turn to," Cheryl snapped. "I hadn't realized you'd become such a little Bolshevik."

"Funny, seeing as how we *all* knew you were always one balcony speech away from going full Evita."

I sat up, again, sidling to the edge of the bunk bed to get back down. "Okay, okay, to your corners, ladies," I said. "For all we know there may be something bucket-esque here, inside. I'll check the—"

Bathroom. I'd been going to say *I'll check the bathroom.*

But before I could get the words out, I was drowned out by the sound of another crash. *Thunder*, I thought, dazed, but thunder didn't explain the sudden, searing pain in my shoulder and the small of my back, or the impact of the wind being knocked out of me.

Somebody shrieked. Maybe more than one person. I turned to my left, only to feel a shooting pain in my neck.

"Veronica?" My voice sounded soft to my ears. "How did you . . . how did you get up to my bunk?"

"I didn't," she stammered, after a shocked beat. "Your bunk . . . it collapsed!"

"Holy crap, Betty! Are you okay?" Toni had leaped from her own bed and hovered over us, concern in her deep brown eyes. "That was insane."

I gaped at the pile of twisted metal and mattresses below me. A few screws and bolts that had been dislodged in the crash were still spinning slowly across the dusty floor. "I think I'm okay," I said. "Although I'm kinda hoping that's the last accident I'm in today."

"We really need to get you a good once-over from Coach Grappler," Toni said, worried.

"Assuming she makes it here," I said. Given the way the storm seemed to be intensifying rather than dying down, I was starting to have serious doubts. What if she never showed up at all?

The thought was too unsettling. I pushed it aside.

"B—you're bleeding," Veronica said, pointing to a thin trail of blood snaking down my forearm.

"It's . . . I mean, it doesn't look deep," I said, dismissive. In truth, looking at the bright red blood was making me a little woozy, but I really didn't want to make a whole thing about it.

"Given that our trained medical professional is somewhere out there, flailing about in the storm, I don't think we can afford to make casual assessments," she said.

"Meaning?"

"Meaning . . . I think I should head to the infirmary and try to find a first aid kit. If nothing else, we can put some antibacterial cream on that arm and bandage it up."

I held my hand to the wound, pressing down and pretending I didn't feel my pulse throbbing beneath my skin. "You're definitely overreacting. But if you *must* go, I'm coming with you."

Veronica narrowed her epic eyebrows my way. "Unacceptable," she said, hands on her hips.

"I'm fine, just sore," I said. "I can make it to the infirmary."

"Of that I've no doubt, my resilient cousin," Cheryl put in, looking at Veronica. "It's no use arguing with you, I can see. Here—" She reached into her pocket and pulled out a familiar-looking square of paper, soggy and waterlogged. "There's a map I found when we were at reception. You can see—the infirmary is down the main trail and then to the right, where there's a bend by . . . I think that's a pagoda?"

I glanced at the map. It was spare, borderline sketch quality, but I got the gist. There was just the one main path, anyway, so it'd be hard to get *too* turned around.

That's what I *thought*, anyway. What I *hoped*.

"I'd like to go on record as saying that I think Betty should stay behind," Veronica said firmly.

"Duly noted, and dismissed accordingly. Godspeed, fair Vixen warriors," Cheryl said. "Oh, and try to be back quickly. There's an"—she made a sour face—"*itinerary* here that Lizzie gave me that indicates an alarming amount of mandated 'fun-tivities' on the docket, and we wouldn't want you to miss any of the excitement. Off you go, the both of you." She waved a hand at us. "And do be dears—keep an eye out for a bucket we might put to use, on your way?"

CHAPTER THIRTEEN

❄ RIVW WEATHER   1 min. ago

Breaking news from the RIVW hot desk: Another security
camera outage has been reported at the Main Street
Small-Mart convenience store. Though store managers are
not claiming any theft or missing inventory, citizens are urged
to use extra caution and to be on alert, particularly during the
storm, as vandals and would-be thieves may be emboldened
by the chaos caused by the extreme weather. Please tune in
for ongoing coverage and further updates. We care about
your safety!

—RIVW.com and affiliates

ʌʌʌ

VERONICA

"What do you suppose the opposite of a rain dance is, Betty?
Can we do one of those?" I mused.

I squeezed Betty's hand, feeling raindrops squelch through
our linked fingers, but my comment didn't have its intended
effect of making her laugh. Or, if she did laugh, it was too softly
to be heard over the steady patter of rain, which had at the very

least subsided to a bearable pressure for the time being. Small favors being what they were, this incremental improvement in our situation was nonetheless still very much appreciated.

"Maybe later," she replied, trying to keep a smile on her face even though I could see she was hating this trek as much as I was.

Betty and I walked in tandem on the muddy path, our flashlights carving bright arcs of light in the murky night sky. Out here at the campgrounds, the sky was studded with stars—the atmosphere, overall, far brighter than we knew even in small-town Riverdale—but we were still deep in the woods, deep within a storm. Which was to say: There probably wasn't enough starlight in the world to make this walk less eerie.

I let go of her fingers and linked my arm through Betty's at the elbow. "I have a fabulous suggestion. What do you say, after this weekend, we put a moratorium on creepy weekends in the woods? I think we've had enough rural noir to last ourselves a short lifetime, don't you think?"

"Right?" Betty echoed, widening her eyes. "It's a deal," she promised. "I was just thinking almost exactly that, earlier, when we were first hiking here—like, when was the last time anything good happened to any of us in the woods?"

"I'd have to cast my mind back to childhood memories at Shadow Lake," I said, considering it. "But even that's probably less than accurate. Think about it—knowing what we do about my father, how unlikely is it that those 'family vacations' of my youth that I recall so fondly were *really* just innocent getaways?"

Thankfully, Betty recognized the rhetorical question for what it was and didn't bother with any meaningless platitudes about my parents only wanting what was best for me and so forth. If anyone "got" what it was like to have shady parents setting questionable examples on the regular, it was the Black Hood's daughter.

"Okay," she said, coming to some sort of decision in her head. "Well, obviously, what we have to do is make a new in-the-woods memory. Fresh start. Wipe the slate clean. If anyone can do it, it's us. We'll salvage this weekend somehow."

"I like the way you think, girl," I said. "But I have to say, we're off to an inauspicious start. The storm, getting run off the road, and then that accident with the bunk bed." I ticked off the laundry list of misfortunes that had plagued us since we first set out on this trip. "It's like Riverdale rules follow us wherever we go."

"Well, I mean, there's that. But you know the saying—bad things happen in threes. That was three. We're done. So maybe now things will turn around?" Even in the dark, I could *feel* Betty shrugging, and I could tell from her tone that she didn't believe her words any more than I did.

Suddenly, Betty jumped, stumbling on the path and pulling me back with her. She gasped. "Did you see that?" Her fingers dug deep into my arms.

I swung my flashlight around with my free hand, right to left, straining my eyes to see. "I see literally nothing but trees, dirt, and puddles. What did *you* see?"

"I'm . . . not sure," she said slowly, rattled.

"I thought . . ." She trailed off. "Never mind. I'm going crazy."

"I mean, it's been a day, and you've had not one but two minor head injuries," I said. "*No one* would fault you for seeing shadows."

"I guess," she said. But she didn't sound convinced. "Oh—wait. That must be it—the infirmary." She tilted her flashlight up so the beam landed squarely on yet another of this place's seemingly infinite ramshackle structures, this one slightly larger than the cabins, with a small, screened-in porch out front. Like nearly all the other buildings on the campgrounds, this one was completely dark.

"It looks deserted," I said, somewhat unnecessarily. "I mean, I know Coach Grappler said her friends were letting us use this space as a favor. And the other squads are apparently chaperone-free. But it feels weird, doesn't it? Us being so completely alone out here?"

"It does," Betty said. "I really hope Coach Grappler's okay. And that she gets here soon."

"Seriously. And not only because, until she does, Cheryl's going all in on her benevolent dictatorship."

"Don't remind me," Betty said. She walked a few feet

forward. "We're here, so I guess we should . . . go in? Look around?" She beckoned to me and then stepped through the door, scrabbling at the wall beside the doorway in search of a light switch.

"Aha!" she said at last, triumphant, and I heard a muted *click* as she flicked the switch.

"Or, semi-*aha*," she amended as the room was suddenly lit in a low, jaundiced hue from a weak, bare bulb swinging from a string in the middle of the ceiling. "That was . . . less helpful than I expected it to be. This place is *really* not into electricity."

"And this infirmary—which feels like a generous term—is more deserted than the so-called welcome office was," I observed, pacing the room. A small desk sat against the back wall facing the front entrance, obviously intended as a reception area. But the desk was streaked with dust and grime and looked like it hadn't seen much use since the last summer season, at best.

"You know," I said, "this place isn't exactly feeling . . . *lively*, given that it's actually a functional, operating summer camp every season. Shouldn't it look a little more lived-in? And a little less . . . decrepit?"

"I'm not gonna argue that," Betty said. "If nothing else, no one's given those bunk beds a once-over in a while, right? And look—more cobwebs." She pointed to another doorway to the side of the reception desk—presumably leading to the dorms where the sickbeds were kept. "Even for a *camp* in the wilderness, this place is definitely feeling rough. I mean . . . someone knew we were coming, right? Someone put together those cabin assignments and the itinerary and stuff. Maybe not for us, since we were so last-minute, but for the Ravenettes? And the Queens? But they still couldn't be bothered to fix the leak in our bunk? Or even, I don't know, run a dust cloth over the place?"

"I guess I just assumed this was what we'd bought into when we'd agreed to do the 'camp retreat' thing in the first place," I said, giving the seemingly deserted cabin another skeptical look. "Leaks. Dust. Insects."

"I mean . . . yeah, there's definitely a certain amount of . . . wilderness you can expect in a wilderness retreat, sure," Betty said, still turning and scanning the place with the precision of a forensics expert. "But this feels . . . a little beyond. Like maybe borderline negligent."

"You're not wrong," I said, taking it all in. "That said . . ."

I trailed off, cocking my head to one side. "It could be some total aural hallucination, or maybe I'm just losing my mind, or god knows what else, after the day from hell we've had . . . but . . . Listen."

Now Betty tilted her head, too, squinting in concentration. A flicker of realization passed over her face, her eyes going wide for a moment, and I knew she'd heard what I'd heard: nothing distinct, nothing so obvious as a person moving around in the building. But *movement* nonetheless, muffled and indistinct. Murmuring. Maybe a voice. Maybe more than one.

Who's here? My belly tightened.

No one, was what we'd been told. And that was odd, all things considered.

But this was odder. And exponentially scarier, too.

Wordlessly, Betty grabbed my hand. Together, we tiptoed past the reception desk and back toward the rear of the building.

ᴧᴧᴧ

The lighting in the dorm room of the infirmary was every bit as "atmospheric" as it had been in the reception office, with the added benefit of wooden-shuttered windows casting moody, menacing shadows along the walls. The room *looked* empty, but still, it felt as though we weren't alone. I couldn't quite say why, only that there was an energy in the air that, coupled with the murmurs we'd heard, seemed potent, almost tactile.

Betty dropped to her knees and began searching under the beds one by one. In here, it was all singles—no bunks. I suppose it would have been too much to ask someone convalescing to hoist themselves up to a top bunk in their weakened state.

She reached her flashlight out to get a better look. Meanwhile, I peered behind anything else I could—a small, rickety chest of drawers against the wall, a few low nightstands made of flimsy plywood that had seen better days. She stood up, dusted off her pants, and we exchanged a look: *nothing*.

Eyes darting around the room, Betty cocked her head toward one last door. It was at the very back, and whatever it housed was as dimly lit as the rest of the space. But as we nodded to each other and crept closer, one thing was unmistakable: The sounds we'd heard in reception were growing louder.

They *were* murmurs. Whispers. Which meant they were probably people.

Tensing, Betty grabbed at the first—and only—thing available to grab, a small table lamp with a ceramic base somewhat listlessly adorning one of the nightstands. It wasn't quite a weapon, but it felt better than going into that small, dark room empty-handed.

Betty motioned for me to get behind her. Together, we tiptoed forward.

At the doorway, though, the murmurings gave way to something more distinct, something louder.

Footsteps.

There was someone in that room.

Before I could even fully process what was happening, the footsteps morphed from sound to movement, an amorphous cloud of shape, lumbering, looming, and opaque. I watched as Betty's fingers tightened around the lamp and she raised it overhead, the muscles in her shoulders quivering and taut. She pulled back with the lamp, ready to bring it down on whoever—*whatever*—was moving toward us . . .

"What the *actual* hell?"

It wasn't a whatever; it was Stasia. She was with another Stonewall Prep girl, the shorter one with the corkscrew curls she wore in buns on either side of her head, peeking up like ears.

"Sorry! I'm—sorry." Betty stepped back, letting the lamp fall limply to her side. Her shoulders slumped, and she looked confused and embarrassed.

I knew the feeling. My cheeks were flaming redder than Cheryl Blossom's signature lipstick, though that was definitely due to how fast my heart was racing from the perceived threat. It would take a hot minute to come down from this.

"We—we heard something, and it was so dark. We were just freaked out. Sorry," I said, taking deep breaths as I spoke. "This must seem insane. We didn't mean to sneak up on you." Another thought occurred to me, though, as soon as I'd gotten the requisite apology out.

"Although . . . what the hell were *you* doing, hiding out here in the dark, anyway?"

"*You* guys are here," not-Stasia retorted.

"Yeah," Betty said, throwing some serious side eye, "but *we're* not *lurking* in the dark in . . . the bathroom? We came to get some bandages, which has to be at least ten times more legit than whatever *you're* doing."

"Not that it's any of your business," not-Stasia said, tilting her chin up defiantly, "but we just needed a place to confer. The bunk's so crowded, there's no privacy. Stasia and I needed a mo'."

Betty raised an eyebrow. "And if we asked you what, exactly, you needed a *mo'* for?"

"Megan and I would kindly remind you that *that's* none of your business, either," Stasia said sweetly. She capped a red Sharpie she was holding at her side and shoved it into the pocket of her jeans without breaking eye contact.

I folded my arms across my chest, glaring. But what could I say? It absolutely *wasn't* our business. No matter *how* sketchy it *definitely* was.

Betty grabbed my arm. "You're right. Sorry about that. No harm, no foul?"

Stasia shrugged. "Whatever."

"And, uh, sorry for almost braining you with a lamp," Betty added, though I could hear the undertone in her voice, the unspoken, *Sorry not sorry, you complete and total freaks.*

"What*ever*," Megan said, echoing Stasia. "It is what it is. We're fine. But you should be getting your Band-Aids or whatever, and getting back. We're supposed to be down at the campfire pit in like twenty."

I glanced out the window, where the wind lashed tree boughs and pounding rain against the screen. "Campfire?"

Stasia gave me a narrow-eyed gaze. "We'll figure out a plan B."

"Excellent," Betty said, short. She led me back through the dorm and past reception, grabbing a stocked first aid kit from a shelf along the way, and both of us stepped out into the wet chill of proper nighttime with a deep breath in unison.

"She's right, unfortunately," Betty said, once we were by ourselves again. "It really *is* none of our business why the hell they're being so weird."

I looked at Betty, seeing the gleam in her eye even by the dim light of the moon. "Girl, you've got a look on your face."

She laughed. "Well. I mean . . . just because it's none of our business . . . that doesn't mean I'm not curious, does it?"

"Curiosity killed the cat, B," I reminded her.

"Maybe," she said. "But that's not going to stop me from keeping an eye out."

I laughed. "Honestly, from you? I'd expect nothing less."

CHAPTER FOURTEEN

ARCHIE

Still feeling lucky?

Kevin Keller's shaky voice echoed in the deep black of the speakeasy.

All around me, I heard chairs scraping against the floor as people jumped up, startled and disoriented. Muffled murmurs floated from every corner.

"Crap!"

"What's going on?"

"What *is* this?"

"I can't find my phone!"

That last one was Sweet Pea, his voice sounding as nervous as Kevin's had.

"Priorities, man." That was a female voice—Peaches, probably. She and Sweet Pea had really been on each other all night, even though the last thing we needed at this exact minute was petty bickering. "You really need to be sending out some texts right about now?"

"It has a *flashlight*," Sweet Pea snapped back. "Which—I don't know if you've realized—in what seems to be a blackout, could actually be pretty helpful."

Even in the dark, I could *feel* the tension building, all thick, like something you could touch. "Guys," I said, trying to project my voice and not sound like I was a little bit freaked by the whole situation myself. "Everyone calm down. It's just a power outage. It'll be over before we know it."

A beam of light twinkled on, shining across the room. It was Jughead, who *did* have his phone and had obviously turned on the flashlight setting. "Everyone's okay, right?"

Before anyone could respond, though, the overhead lights flickered, then lit back up, illuminating the room again. "Well, whatever that was, at least it was quick," I said, relieved.

My relief didn't last long, though. Suddenly, Munroe made a sound—something between a shout and a shocked cry—at my side.

"The—pot." He was pointing, color drained from his face, to the center of our card table. "What the . . . ?"

"Where'd it go?" Jughead asked. He jumped up and pivoted side to side, eyes searching. "This isn't funny, guys!"

"Yo!" Reggie was on his feet, moving back from the bar and to the table, bouncing like a boxer before a match. He looked just as wired—and just as ready to go into the ring with someone. Or maybe with *any*one. *"Who took it?"*

I swallowed, tasting bile, sour at the back of my throat. If this was a prank, it was a lousy one. But if it was something else . . . well, that was definitely much, much worse.

Because the center of that card table? The one where we'd all just bought in to our double-or-nothing, winner-takes-all round?

It was empty.

The money was gone.

My temper flared, almost immediately—along with my suspicions.

Bottom line? I don't trust Reggie.

Not *really*. Even though we're supposed to be friends and stuff. There's just . . . a piece that's always missing. Even if I didn't want it to be that way. For one thing, even as far back as Little League days, he was always crazy about pranks and stuff, like in a way that often went beyond "funny" and cruised straight into "mean." We were always kind of in competition with each other, from getting picked first for dodgeball in second-grade gym class, all the way to clashing over who'd get to be captain of the Bulldogs.

And then there was the whole thing where he hooked up with Veronica for a while last year. I know, I'm supposed to be all mature and enlightened about it—what was she going to do, pine away for me like some character in a soap opera while I was on the run from her father *and* the law? But I guess it turns out I'm not all that enlightened, after all.

I mean yeah, I wanted Veronica to be happy. But did she have to be happy with *Reggie*?

Petty, I know. Petty and dumb—and hypocritical, too.

Especially seeing as how I was dating Josie for a while there myself.

But Reggie. What I'm saying is even though we're sometimes like brothers, Reggie and me, we also fight like brothers. And when push comes to shove? I just can't totally trust him.

Which was why, now that the lights were back on at La Bonne Nuit and we'd all kind of slowly, blearily started to wrap our minds around the fact that the *freaking poker pot was missing*, I immediately got a strong-ass whiff of foul play. And it was coming straight from Reggie—big surprise.

"Did you do it, man?" I demanded, staring at Reggie. "Did you take the pot when the lights were out?"

Reggie held his hands up and stepped back, very dramatically "not me." "Yo, man, are you crazy?"

"No, I just know you. *Well*. And this little stunt has your name written all over it."

Everyone in the speakeasy was pacing, glancing around, obviously considering where the money could be. Tensions were beyond high. Hell—it was a *ton* of cash at stake. And even if no one wanted to admit it, we were definitely still feeling freaked from the blackout and wondering if—and when—it might happen again.

Reggie made an incredulous face. With big, exaggerated movements, he yanked at the lining of his jeans pockets so they poked out, stiff—but empty.

The room was silent, unconvinced but unsure of where to go from here. Finally, Munroe stepped forward. He and Reggie were cool now, but they'd had their history. Munroe was probably thinking of some of that now.

"Cute act, pretty boy," he said, his voice low and gruff. "But I know a con when I see it. So how about you tell us where the money is, or *I'll* have a look in those pockets myself?"

Reggie took his own step forward, so he and Munroe were practically nose to nose. "Are you really gonna go all *Raging Bull* on me, bro?"

"Okay." Jughead moved cautiously, like the guys were rabid, feral creatures he was trying to subdue. "Listen, you two—I like a *Fight Club* reenactment as much as the next borderline antisocial white guy. But this isn't going anywhere good." He put his hands on his hips. "Mantle, you can understand why you might be the prime suspect here?"

Reggie shot him a death glare. "Do you *really* think I'm gonna answer that the way you want me to? I *told* you guys, I didn't do it. I was *winning*. Why would I steal the pot?"

"To make sure your winning streak doesn't end," I snapped.

"And I do hear you, Arch," Jughead interjected. "I'm saying, we don't *need* to rely on mere speculation. Reggie can look at the security footage, right? Like they used to say in the heady heyday of broadcast news: Let's go to tape."

"About that, though," Reggie said, looking uncomfortable.

"What?" I snarled.

He grabbed the tablet off the bar where he'd left it. "I just looked. The cameras are completely down."

Jughead smacked his forehead with his hand. "Because of the blackout. Duh. How did we not think about that?"

"But isn't the tablet also connected to the cell network?" Kevin asked. "That's supposed to be, like, a fail-safe."

"Not if the network is down because of the storm, though," Reggie said.

"What about a backup generator?" I said, looking Reggie squarely in the eyes. "If I know Veronica, she would have definitely put one of those in place."

For a second, it looked like Reggie was faltering. I'll admit, I kind of liked seeing it.

"Uh, it doesn't switch on until the power's been down for thirty minutes," he said, hesitant. "If it kicked on for every little outage it would run out of juice before a real emergency."

Jughead looked suspicious. "I thought you said earlier that the whole point of the system was that it was *all* automatic? That it 'kicks on' no matter what?"

"God, okay. Nice third degree, man," Reggie said, doing his best "casual." I noticed he didn't actually answer the question, though.

Was it just me, or was he basically deflecting, trying to keep us from checking that security-cam footage? A quick glance at

Jughead told me he was thinking the same thing. "That's pretty convenient for you," he commented dryly.

"Well, I mean, seeing as you're all on this crazy witch hunt, it's really *not*," Reggie said. "Here—take a look for yourself."

Jughead grabbed the tablet and beckoned to me. I moved to look over his shoulder. The screen was just a set of schematics of the space, from what I could see. It didn't look like anything.

Reggie was right, though—the camera wasn't recording.

Jughead was frowning at the tablet, tapping at it furiously. "Too bad JB's not here," he mumbled. "She's the one who's really good with these things." He looked up. "But as far as I can tell? Reggie's telling the truth. The whole system is down, including the cameras."

"That's what I've been telling you," Reggie said, exasperated. "And it's super weird. The power's back up, so the cameras should be, too. And so should the door locks. I don't know what's going on."

"Wait, what do you mean?" I asked, uneasy.

"Well . . . the *whole* system is down. Like, all of it. Meaning, the whole speakeasy is in lockdown mode."

There were a few scattered gasps at that.

Kevin gasped. "Why would Veronica even *have* that feature for her system?"

"You know the Lodges love a good panic room," I said. "If the place goes into lockdown when the system goes out, that's what this whole place becomes."

"Great," Kevin said, eyes wide. "My panic feels appropriate, in that case."

"One good thing about the lockdown?" Munroe said. "We can *find the missing money*. It couldn't have gone too far."

Sweet Pea stepped forward, closer to the fray in the center of the room. "Yeah," he said, sounding just slightly too eager about it all. "Serpents are totally representing here. We've worked security at La Bonne Nuit for Veronica in the past. Happy to step up, pat people down, whatever you need."

"Poisons, too," Peaches put in, throwing a dirty look at Sweet Pea.

Jughead turned to Sweet Pea and Peaches, frustrated. "*Seriously?* This noise, *now*?"

"I'm not—" Sweet Pea started, protesting, but Jug held up a hand, cutting him off.

"Do I need to remind you who your Serpent King is?" Jughead asked, quiet.

"Uh, guys," Kevin said, breaking into the loaded silence with as much tact as he could muster, "I think everyone needs to take at least ten deep breaths. Tensions are running a *little* high."

"Oh, you think?" Chuck asked, taking a big gulp of whatever he was drinking and savoring it, clearly enjoying the show.

"It's totally understandable," Kevin went on. "All that money missing, people have been drinking . . . And then there's the fact that we're all stuck down here—sealed up, underground, all alone, while a storm rages outside. Isn't that, like, a classic recipe for any number of cinematic-scale disasters?"

I opened my mouth to respond—he definitely had a point, though it wasn't exactly doing much to calm me down— but before I could, I heard a weird noise. A creaking. Like someone—or *more* than one someone—on the stairs to the speakeasy.

We all turned to the entrance to the room in unison, like we were somehow automatically programmed to move that way. And all together, we gasped when we realized just what we were looking at.

"Don't worry," Dodger said, grinning at us with satisfaction. He stood at the bottom of the staircase, a line of his crew all crowded together on the stairs in one big clump behind him.

"You're *not* all alone down here anymore."

CHAPTER FIFTEEN

CHERYL

"I'm sorry, is that meant to be a split-sit? Because from this vantage point, it better resembles my sorrel roan when she was plagued with intestinal parasites." I bit my lip. "To further clarify: *That* wasn't pretty. And neither is this."

Ambiguity is for losers, after all.

The itinerary we'd all seen had dictated that we should meet at the campfire, ostensibly for marshmallow-roasting and the singing of "Kumbaya." But given that the storm made that beyond impossible, we had collectively determined to move to the next thing on the list: cheer drills, with the mess hall filling in for the practice field, because, again, storm.

I suppose the theory was that we'd learn and grow from one another's techniques and routines, and other such stuff and nonsense. But I sincerely doubted that either the Queens or the Ravenettes had any superior skills worth passing along; and I'd eat my red-checked hunting cap before I'd give away any of our own hard-earned trade secrets. But nevertheless, the schedule was what it was, and it's not like we had anything better to do. Plus, at least the mess hall was leak-free (Betty and Veronica's search for a bucket on their return from the infirmary had been less than fruitful), and it gave us some access to sustenance. And it just so happened that people were famished after our arduous journey.

So here we were now, watching with barely veiled boredom as the Ravenettes demonstrated their latest stunt. Color me *un*impressed.

I cast my most withering gaze at them, directing the bulk of my disdain at the one they called Jules, a flier slathered in more pancake makeup than a common Parisian street mime. "I ask you: What has become of the governing guidelines of our sport? Aren't there meant to be dress codes for competition cheer squads?" I stage-whispered to Toni. "Codes that *preclude* such tacky and tasteless modes of self-expression?"

"Well, yeah . . . I think so," she whispered back. "But they *might* also 'preclude' dyed hair in bright colors like mine, so maybe let's not pull at that thread right now?" She flipped the vivid bubblegum tips of her twin braids at me, pleading playfully.

I squeezed her hand. "Understood, *mon petit trésor*." Not that the guidelines ever applied to me or my own, but her point was well enough taken. I leaned in for a kiss.

"Hey! Maybe a little bit less with the PDA and a little more running through these drills with the group—in a *constructive* way?"

"Explain yourself, shrew," I spat reflexively.

I looked up to see Lizzie glaring at me, tapping her foot. "Look, *I* didn't make the schedule, and *god* knows, the last thing I'm interested in is a series of 'funtivities' and trust-building exercises with . . . you all." She wrinkled her nose, as though *we* were the ones figuratively raining all over what had been billed as an exclusive weekend. "But we *are* here for a reason."

Indeed, we were, though I'd been doing my damnedest to forget that reason from the moment we arrived to find these haggard interlopers disrupting what was meant to be a serene—and solitary—retreat. (The rain being both figurative *and* literal, my leadership skills were being put to the utmost test.)

"Sorry, ladies," I said, not bothering to stifle a yawn. "But until you can show me something more challenging than those amateur-hour stunts we Vixens were doing back when we were still mere young JV whippersnappers, I think I'll stick to sneaking stolen moments with *mon petit bijou*." I paused, considering. "No, wait—actually, I'm not sorry at all."

"Nice," Lizzie said, signaling to her squad that they could begin to dismount. She swiped her forearm across her forehead, wiping away a sheen of sweat. "Well, given that you guys are so advanced, maybe you could show us some of your rock-star moves." She put her hands on her hips. "Anytime you're ready."

"Must we?" I sighed. "As much as I'd love to show you all what a *real* cheer squad can do, it's been a long, grueling day. In addition to the crash that took us off the road on the way here, Betty"—I swept my arm out, gesturing grandly—"was injured in our cabin. Her bunk bed collapsed; it was truly calamitous. And though she's fine, I'd say we're all a bit worse for the wear."

Betty shifted in her seat, looking curious. "Hey, wait," she started. "Back up. If you guys didn't make the activities schedule"—she looked at Lizzie—"then who did?"

Lizzie squinted at her, confused. "What?"

Betty stood now. "Who made the schedules?" she repeated, enunciating more clearly and insistently this time. "You got a copy in the welcome office. But there was no one *in* the office . . . and there's no one here now. So, where did it come from?"

"Thank god you're on the case, Nancy Drew," Megan, the squat, unfortunate-looking cheerleader whose *raison d'être* appeared to be nipping at Stasia's heels like a poorly trained puppy, chimed in with an eye roll. "I mean, all three of our squads were supposed to be here—one way or another—this weekend. Someone knew that. And that someone—most likely, whoever manages the camp's administrative stuff—knew and put together a little itinerary for us. Just because they're not here now doesn't make it, like, deep-state subterfuge."

Betty was obviously unconvinced. "It still seems weird. You said yourself, your coaches assumed there would be people in charge here. But there's no staff; there was no one *in* the welcome office when we got here . . ."

"Simmer down," Stasia put in. "Maybe you're just weak

with hunger or fatigue, but you're seeing conspiracy theories where there clearly are none, and honestly? It's a little embarrassing. We used to come to this place every year for a retreat. We know it like the back of our hands. The owners must have just known we didn't need a whole lot of hand-holding."

"You *used* to come." Betty tilted her head, thinking.

"Yeah," Stasia said, suddenly looking uncertain.

"And you guys, too?" Betty glanced at the Ravenettes.

"It was a tradition for a while," Lizzie said.

"But then the tradition ended?" Veronica asked, arching an eyebrow.

Lizzie's expression hardened. "It happens. Traditions end," she said, her voice flat. "And then the owners invite you back one year, because they miss you. I don't know, it's not like it's a whole big thing. I don't know why you have to make it out like it is."

Veronica tossed her head so her jet-black waves bounced. "You guys are being mighty dismissive of something that's downright shady. Fact: None of us know *who,* exactly, created those schedules for us." She held one manicured finger up, as though kicking off a countdown.

"*You* all may think it's NBD," she went on. "But those of us who are coming of age in Riverdale understandably have our doubts. In our shockingly high-drama adolescent experience, where there's sketchy smoke? There's fire. Generally a veritable inferno of it."

"Good thing it's way too wet for fire tonight, then," Stasia said, smirking. "But points for being so extra. We'll be sure to submit this clip for your Emmy reel, girlfriend."

"And I guess neither of you wants to elaborate on why your traditional retreats ended?" Betty asked.

"Maybe we just don't need to cater to your third degree," Lizzie said. "We're here now. New beginnings and all that."

Toni stepped forward. "You know," she mused, "*if* the fact that we're totally unsupervised here is shady—"

"It's not." Lizzie rolled her eyes.

"Then maybe Betty's broken bunk bed is shady, too."

Stasia put her hands on her hips. "Now you're just grasping at straws. It's an old camp."

"An old camp that's trying to encourage people to reembrace old traditions," Veronica countered. "So you'd think they'd be motivated to make sure the cabins were in tip-top shape. And, I don't know, have some staff on-site? Or at least run a dust cloth over the place."

"You said yourself that your coach knows the owners and reached out to them last-minute," Stasia said. "I guess they assumed she'd take care of things here."

Betty frowned. I could tell she was trying to temper her own concerns about Coach Grappler. It *was* starting to feel like a minute since we'd last seen her . . .

I jumped in. "Suffice it to say, we Vixens will keep our wits about us, and keep a sharp eye out until we're certain that everything is on the up-and-up here at Sweetwater Pines. Let it not be said that we don't learn from past experiences. And while your blasé response to our harrowing journey here, not to mention Betty's near-death experience in our cabin—"

"I wouldn't say—" Betty tried to interject, but I held up a hand and raised my voice, plowing ahead with determined aplomb.

"While your total apathy with regards to our personal, physical peril is observed and noted for posterity, as captain of this squad, I'm making the executive decision that effective immediately, all stunt drills will be placed on hold until my girls have had something to eat."

A few scattered cheers around me told me that the Vixens were pleased with this decree. Frankly, it should have occurred to me sooner, but I suppose the dire straits of our stormy afternoon could be considered extenuating circumstances. Meaning: My small misstep was fully understandable in the context of the day we'd had.

"Eat?" Megan echoed, wrinkling her brow like I'd suggested ritual sacrifice or a suicide pact. "Eat what?"

"I have some protein bars in the cabin!" the decidedly malnourished Jules put in, her enthusiasm at odds with her wan, emo aesthetic.

"Sounds delish," I said, curling my lip in distaste. "But my fellow brethren: Need I point out that we are currently standing *in the camp mess hall*? Surely we can find some more appealing option."

"I don't know, Cheryl," Ginger said. "Camp food is, like, notoriously gross."

"In that case, *you* don't have to eat it," I snapped. "But something tells me we can find *something* snackable in that industrial-sized kitchen.

"This is a challenge, squads," I said grandly, sweeping my arm out and leading them in the direction of the kitchen. "But surely we are women up to a challenge."

∧∧∧

In truth, it was slim pickings. Or rather, the quantity of food was abundant, to be sure, even in the off-season. But the quality left quite a bit to be desired—even for those of us who weren't necessarily accustomed to the luxuries of life at Thistlehouse. In the end, we settled on the classic but unassailable PB&J—basic, yes, but archetypical for a reason. Toni dug up some mini cartons of chocolate milk like you might get at preschool snack time, which felt surprisingly comforting in the moment. Tina grabbed a few bags of off-brand potato chips, and we settled in around the dining tables, more nourished by the simple snack than I think any of us would have actually cared to admit.

For a time, we ate in companionable (enough) silence. But

once we'd subdued the most pressing of our hunger pangs, a slow, cautious conversation couldn't help but begin to unfold.

"So," Lizzie started, running her finger around the edge of her sandwich to catch a trail of strawberry jam runoff, "you weren't impressed by our stunt." She looked at me, challenging.

I shrugged. "I understand—the truth hurts. But indeed, it's a stunt we Vixens have literally been performing for eons. It was the first one I learned when I joined the JV squad—that wasn't an exaggeration." Far be it from me to pull my punches; anyone who knows me would be the first to reiterate that.

"It's the truth," Betty said, jumping in. While I certainly didn't *need* her validation, I'll confess it was nice to feel supported.

Stasia turned to Lizzie. "Sorry, but a split-sit *is* pretty much amateur hour, especially if you're doing the competition circuit."

Lizzie glared at her. "As if *you* guys can even touch us when it comes to 'the competition circuit.'" She rolled her eyes. "Your jealousy is understandable, but it's not a good look, Queenie. Thank you, next."

She narrowed her eyes at me now, obviously out for blood. Or at the very least, out to make me squirm after putting her on the spot. I didn't blame her in the least. I would have done the same. "So, what's your most advanced stunt, then? Since you're such full-on pros?"

I drummed my fingers on the table, pretending to think it over. *Please.* There was only one response to such a challenge. "Wolf wall," I said, flashing a self-satisfied grin. "It was our halftime finale at the last homecoming, and it also fetched us the title at the All River Valley Invitational last spring."

Lizzie remained impressively stoic, but Stasia gave a low whistle, unable to feign nonchalance at that. And with good reason: A wolf wall is notoriously one of the most advanced cheer stunts allowed in competition. It was a lift, albeit a deceptively elaborate one at that—an intricate pyramid. And while pyramids may look static, the fact is that they're actually one continuous train of stunting activity, a dizzying combo of lifts, poses, and dismounts. Ours was two-and-a-half high, the maximum allowed in competition (and even prohibited in certain competitions due to an alarming number of undertrained squads undertaking the feat, to ghastly outcomes).

Poor, doomed Midge Klump had been our center flier once, before her gruesome and untimely death; she was lithe and toned, which made her that magical combination of impossibly strong yet disarmingly easy to lift. These days, Toni had taken her place, and while I missed Midge dreadfully and meant no disrespect to her memory, I had to say that my TeeTee was taking up the mantle quite admirably.

(*Quelle surprise.* No—I jest, of course. Nothing about Toni Topaz surprises me other than her stunning ability to continue to scale new levels of near-divine perfection.)

"You'll have to show us later, after we've all finished eating and digested and stuff," Stasia went on. "I mean, a wolf wall is the stuff of legends. I heard a squad from Centerville tried it at nationals one year, and their best flier ended up in a coma." She shuddered at the thought.

Ginger snorted. "I mean, would you expect anything else from *Centerville*?" She sounded callous, to be sure, but they were our most bitter rivals, and her sentiment was widely held among the team. Not to mention, I'd heard the same story, only in my case it was the Peeksville Wildcats, and the flier had ended up paralyzed, not in a coma. In other words, the provenance of the story was suspect at best.

"Mayhap we can share a few of our lesser trade secrets," I said, short. "That is, *if* we're feeling generous of spirit. I can't make any promises. Keep in mind, none of us are at our best just now. As I've mentioned, poor Betty has been injured twice over, despite your steadfast refusal to demonstrate a modicum of concern for her well-being." *Speaking* of craven and callous . . .

"I'm sorry, what exactly did you want us to do about it?" Lizzie asked. "No one here is, like, a medical professional."

"Exactly," Veronica chimed in. "And given that harsh reality, while it may seem excessive, may I propose an abundance of caution going forward? For the time that we're here on our own, that is. Save the stunts and other feats of physical prowess for when Coach Grappler gets here."

"*If* your coach gets here, you mean," Lizzie scoffed.

Betty gave her a look. "She'll be here."

Lizzie shrugged. "Think about it: It's storming. She's not here yet. You can probably do the math." She exchanged a knowing look with Jules. "I mean, I don't blame you for holding out hope, but her making it here tonight is feeling pretty optimistic, if you ask me."

"Which we didn't," I reminded her. "But I'll be sure to file your input away for future reference, should the need arise."

"It's a mess out there," Betty protested. "I'm sure she's still just waiting on Triple B."

"Of course she is. In the meantime," Veronica said, a sly grin creeping across her face, "how about we put aside these petty rivalries, forget about all the banal 'team-building' stuff that was written into the itinerary, and just have, you know, *fun*?" She looked around, her face open and hopeful. "No more of this 'East Coast/West Coast' style old-school rivalry—pun not intended. You guys *do* remember fun, right?"

As a matter of fact, I did. And what Veronica was proposing did sound promising. Glancing around the room, I could tell from the looks on everyone's faces that I wasn't the only one who felt that way.

"What did you have in mind?" Stasia asked.

"Nothing too elaborate," Veronica said. "No need to reinvent the wheel. It's basically little more than a large-scale slumber party here, right? So how about some party games?"

"Ooh," I said, warming to the idea. "What about a round of secrets and sins?" *I'm in the mood for chaos.* That was my credo, after all. When was it not true?

Veronica made a face. "That game is straight-up toxic," she protested. "Not to mention, no offense, Cheryl, but it's really just saying mean things about each other. There's no actual game to it."

"Fine," I said, short. "What do you propose instead?"

"Let's start simply," Veronica said. "Truth or dare."

$\sim\sim\sim$

Secrets and sins may have had less nuance to it, but truth or dare wasn't exactly wholesome family fun, either. At least, not the way *we* played it. We pushed the dining tables out of the way, clearing a space in the center of the floor so we could sit in a circle, like we would have if we'd been able to perch down at the fire pit in the first place. Someone dimmed the lights, casting an eerie, atmospheric pall over the room that wasn't totally unwelcome.

"So," Betty said, once we'd all assembled ourselves and were ready to dive into the juicy stuff. "Who goes first?" She reached up and yanked at her ponytail, tightening it even higher on her head, like she was preparing to get down to some serious business and not a round of a silly teen-party game.

Megan grinned, a slow, rubbery look that inched across

her face in a way that managed to seem more creepy than happy. "I think the one who brought the party favors gets first crack."

"Party favors?" Toni glanced at her, questioning.

By way of response, Megan reached into her warm-up jacket, pulling something out of an inner pocket. It was a flask, I realized—something polished and silver and etched with a detailing I didn't recognize. My dearly departed Jay-Jay had carried one just like it, to tailgates and summer weekend cookouts. I doubted it was filled with lemonade (Jay-Jay's never was)—and I didn't mind one bit.

"Is there even enough in there for all of us?" Jules broke in, snide.

Megan looked at her, impassive. "There's more where this one came from. Back in the bunk. Don't sweat it."

"It's pouring out," Jules protested. "No one's gonna want to go all the way back to the bunk for a refill."

"Well, then, I guess we'll just have to *dare* someone to do it," I snapped. "Honestly, have you *zero* imagination?"

"Let's press pause on that particular conversation," Veronica suggested, holding up one hand. "Back to the matter at hand: the game. I think we can agree that if you're providing refreshments, Megan, you've earned the right to go first." Veronica surveyed the group, taking in our nods of agreement. She held out her arm, as if in deference. "Take it away."

"Okay," Megan said, shimmying a little in her seat as she

considered her move. Then she turned to Stasia, her gaze laser-sharp. "Stasia: truth or dare?"

Stasia rolled her eyes. "Ugh, this game is so ridiculous. *We're classmates*, need I remind you? We're on the same team." Megan was impassive.

Stasia shook her head. Obviously, no one was going to let her off the hook. "Whatever. Truth, I guess."

"Nice," Megan said approvingly. She gave a wicked, crooked smile. "Truth: Have you now, or have you ever, had a crush on a former Riverdale High student?"

Whoa. Talk about chaos. I guess I wasn't the only one who liked a little bit of hell-raising every now and then.

Stasia made a face like she'd just smelled something foul and shot Megan a dirty look. Meanwhile, everyone in the room whipped around, practically in unison, to observe Betty's reaction to the question. To her credit, she was staring straight ahead, gaze fixed, though the slight tinge of pink to her cheeks and the mild twitch of her forehead threatened to give her away. Betty and I may not have been bosom buddies, but I knew my cousin: Her darker half was bubbling to the surface. I wondered if she'd be able to keep it at bay.

"I'm sorry, is this truth or dare, or the McCarthy hearings?" Stasia sniped, deflecting. Around her, girls wagged their eyebrows, registering her reluctance to respond.

"That's totally not an answer to the question," Megan

pointed out, undeterred. She took a swig from her flask and passed it to Stasia. "Here. Truth serum, if you need a boost."

Stasia narrowed her eyes at Megan even further, if that were even possible, but then leaned to grab the flask from her, taking a long pull. "Yes," she said at last, swallowing loudly. She looked at Betty. "I have."

Betty met Stasia's gaze but said nothing. For a moment, the tension in the room was mud thick. Then a wave of tittering broke out, nervous and tinny and high.

"*OMG, so awkward*," Ginger whispered, though her whisper was louder than most people's speaking voices and not at all discreet.

No one spoke for a beat, everyone shifting nervously, waiting for the giggles to die down and glancing with desperate longing at the flask.

"Fine," I said, breaking the stony silence. "While I do love a bout of chaos, Ginger is right. This is *très* awkward. Let's move on. I volunteer as tribute."

"No," Betty said, leaning in to the circle. "I've got a truth for Stasia."

"Excuse me, but double jeopardy," Stasia said. "If you want the DL on my *minor-league* feels for your bae, you'll have to get it later. But I promise you, the infatuation was short-lived. That guy is embarrassingly hooked on you."

Betty's eyes flashed, her expression inscrutable. "That's not what I was going to ask about." She shifted, her gaze landing on Lizzie. "But I can ask you, instead. Lizzie, truth: Why did your team stop coming to Sweetwater Pines?"

Lizzie groaned. "Oh my *god*, are you one of those, like, total conspiracy theorists? Do you belong to secret chat rooms about how the moon landing was faked? *It's. Nothing.* Once upon a time, our squad used to come here. Then they didn't. The end." She folded her arms over her chest. "What can I say? This place went downhill. When we got invited back, we were hopeful they'd gotten their act together." She sniffed. "But apparently not."

"*Went downhill* as in . . ." Betty prodded.

"There were . . . accidents," Lizzie said with a forced air of vagueness. "Really, you should ask Stasia. Something weird is always going on with those Stonewall kids. Missing students and whatever. It's like their *thing*."

"*Enough!*" Stasia said. "This is pointless. And we're not even sticking to the rules of the game."

"There are *rules* to this nonsense?" Toni asked, incredulous.

"Cheryl volunteered," Stasia said. "We're getting sidetracked."

"Indeed. Try me," I said.

"Excellent. Truth or dare?" Stasia asked. I detected a note of admiration in her voice. She passed me the flask. "And while you consider: enjoy."

"*Salud*," I said, taking a gulp. I leveled her with a steady gaze. "Dare."

(I *always* choose dare.)

Stasia wrinkled her brow, considering. Before she could say anything, Lizzie cut in.

"I've got a good one!" she said, nodding. "Right outside, there's a set of dumpsters. Maybe empty, I'm not sure. I didn't exactly go out of my way for a close look." She tilted her head, like she wasn't all that concerned either way.

"It's off-season," Veronica said. "No one's even been using this place. They *must* be empty, or relatively empty, anyway."

"*We're* using it this weekend," Lizzie pointed out. "Who's to say that others haven't been as well? Anyway, if they're empty, so be it. You're in luck, Red."

"All right. So, what's the dare, then?" I asked, sighing. "I jump into the dumpster and bathe in the trash like some sort of Dickensian take on a bacchanal?"

Lizzie winked at me. "Close, but no cigar. It'll be much better than that."

"Okay, hang on. I think we need a few ground rules," Toni said, stepping in. "Nothing truly dangerous, and no daring people to ingest anything that could actually make a person sick."

"*Make a person sick* is a pretty broad term, doll face," Lizzie pointed out. "But it's fine, we'll keep it somewhere between a three to five on the proverbial 'mortal danger' spectrum. Okay?"

Reluctantly, Toni nodded, though she looked like she wanted to say more.

Lizzie leaned in, warming to her dare. "So, the dumpsters. They're right outside, through the back exits in the kitchen. *Your* mission, Cheryl, should you choose to accept it"—she smiled—"just kidding, you chose dare, there's no opting out of this one now . . ."

I rolled my eyes so hard I feared they'd fall from my head. "Sweet maple syrup on a corn fritter, woman. For the love of all jubilant jezebels, will you *please* just get on with it?" I folded my arms over my chest, frustrated.

"*Your mission*," she went on smoothly, "is to dig something out of one of the dumpsters that's edible . . . and eat it."

"Repugnant," I said. "And unoriginal." But also easy enough. That was the beauty of these basic prep school drones: no imagination. Low-level harassment? I could handle that. Please—I was practically an expert in such things. Water off the red swan's back.

"Unoriginal, and *also* against the rules I just stated," Toni jumped in. "Nothing that will make someone sick."

"And as *I stated*, 'make someone sick' is a wholly relative phrase. It's up to Cheryl to find something in there that won't result in a need for a trip to the ER."

Jules jumped to her feet, clearly eager to support her friend.

What a well-trained minion, I thought, working to keep a tinge of grudging admiration at bay.

"I mean, there are, like, people who eat that way as a way of life. *On purpose.* They do it on the regular. Freegans, you know?" Jules said.

"I'm familiar with the term," I told her. "And yet somehow, I've never exactly aspired to live my life as a common scavenger."

"Well, there's a first time for everything," Lizzie said. She smiled wide enough that I could see the points of her canine teeth, gleaming and wet. In the murky light of the dining hall, they looked dagger-sharp and vaguely inhuman. She winked again, the movement slow and borderline grotesque. "Get at it, girl," she drawled. "What are you waiting for?"

"Fret not, you harridan," I said. "Cheryl Bombshell's not one to back down from a challenge."

"Great. And pro tip?" she added as I reluctantly rose from the circle and prepared for my personal crucible. "You might want to bring an umbrella."

I didn't bother to dignify the comment with a reply.

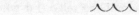

An umbrella, as it turns out, would not have helped matters.

Frankly, I doubt anything less than a fully sealed hazmat suit would have helped matters. (And believe you me, I would have paid a pretty penny for one of those just then. Particularly given that I was about to have an unsolicited up-close-and-personal *rendezvous* with a heaping pile of wet, soggy trash.)

The thunder, at least, had lessened to a respectable, low-key but persistent rumble, but the rain was back on in full force, so heavy that I had to hold a palm up flat against my forehead just to be able to see even a scant few inches in front of my face at a time. Lizzie was right, though, in that the dumpsters were directly outside the mess hall, once you emerged from the kitchen doors, so all I had to do was shuffle a few tentative steps to the right before I hit upon the first one.

(Fortuitous indeed.)

It took two hands to lift the cover, and I tried to avoid the hideous cliché of being the diva who worried about breaking a nail under even the most preposterous circumstances. (Full disclosure: I had a backup bottle of Tom Ford Smoke Red in my duffel back in the bunk, so there was no true danger here. Let it not be said that Cheryl Blossom doesn't come to all situations prepared.) Luckily, my archery prowess had bequeathed me a surprising amount of upper-body strength.

The stench hit first, as the cover hinged up, creaking loudly, engulfing me so that I viscerally recoiled. I'd never encountered anything quite like it—and I'd personally spent several months ensconced in a makeshift tent city with a cadre of vagabond gang members, so this was saying something. I gagged, the little I'd actually eaten today threatening to come up, but with a few slow breaths—mouth only—I was able to calm myself.

Something edible . . . the mere suggestion made my lower

intestines twist again. It was unclear how recently these dumpsters had been in use—did the vile odor indicate more or less? Who could say?—but regardless, I knew there was nothing in here that I would *ever*, under any circumstances, willingly put into my body.

A dare was a dare, though . . . and the only thing I wanted to do even less than see this particular dare to completion was to see the look on Lizzie's face if I failed. There was simply no way I could possibly abide by that. I held my nose, steeled my will, and leaned over the dumpster, plunging my free hand into the great unknown of refuse.

It was only a minute or two later that I began to scream.

CHAPTER SIXTEEN

VERONICA

I was busy trying to decide whether I was surprised that Cheryl actually took the dumpster-dive dare (on the one hand, girl-friend was definitely not the freegan type. On the other, Cheryl Blossom definitely never backed down from a challenge) when I heard it: a scream.

It was shrill and high-pitched, piercing the rhythmic patter of the rainfall and carrying to the main dining room of the mess hall all the way from . . .

"That's out back!" Toni said, jumping up. "That's *Cheryl*!"

"I'm sure she just saw a mouse back there or something," Jules said, unimpressed. "You Vixens need to toughen up."

"Watch it," Ginger started, raring up, but I held her back.

I shot Jules a look of my own. "You'll forgive us if we actually go investigate for ourselves."

"You'd better pray she's okay," Toni said to Lizzie, her gaze cold.

I grabbed Betty's hand and we all raced toward the kitchen, to the back exit of the mess hall, tearing toward the sound of Cheryl's shrieks as fast as we possibly could.

ᴧᴧᴧ

Outside, Cheryl was slumped against one of the dumpsters, her hair plastered to her skull in long, wet straggles. She held something in her hands that I couldn't quite make out, and her expression was one of horror and disbelief. In the storm, it was impossible to tell whether the streaks of water on her face were raindrops or tears, but if I had to guess, I'd say it was likely some combination of both.

"Cheryl!" Toni grabbed her by the shoulders, probably harder than she intended to, but the girl seemed stunned and almost catatonic, so maybe it was necessary.

Slowly Cheryl blinked and looked up. "Oh, hello, TeeTee. Are you here to help with the dare? I must warn you, it's feeling quite pointless, in light of what I've found out here in the process of completing Lizzie's puerile task."

Without answering, Toni just pulled Cheryl into a tight hug.

"What is it?" I asked. "We heard you screaming. What's wrong?"

The question felt woefully inadequate the moment it was out of my mouth. What was wrong? What *wasn't*? But even aggregating all the ways in which this cheer retreat had already gone sideways, I still couldn't account for the bloodcurdling fear we'd heard in Cheryl's voice just now.

Reluctantly, she held her hands up, demonstrating. It took me a minute to even realize exactly what I was looking at.

Beside me, Betty gasped. "Is that—"

"Witchcraft," Cheryl said simply. "Pure and simple."

I didn't know about witchcraft, but what I saw was inarguably creepy: a cluster of Barbie dolls, all different hair and skin tones, naked except for small pom-poms that had been glued to their hands, and stripped of any facial features. Their hair had been chopped into spiky tufts, and they were tied together with grimy twine. And as I examined closer I realized . . .

"Is that *Sharpie*? Over their eyes?" Someone had drawn harsh, jagged X's where the dolls' eyes had once been. The marker was a vivid red, lurid in the gray-tinged night.

"It's a *message,* that's what it is," Cheryl said, grim. "Someone wants to freak us out. And I daresay it's beginning to work."

"We don't know that it was meant for us," I protested.

"Actually," Betty said, "these dolls may have been in the trash, but they weren't there for long. They're pretty clean."

We all took a closer look, shivering. She was right.

"And if these were meant for us"—she looked at us, her mouth twisting in worry—"I have to wonder if the broken bunk bed was actually meant for us, too."

We all fell silent, considering this.

Toni looked at her. "So, you don't think that was an accident?"

Betty shrugged. "I don't know what to think. Everything about this place feels . . . off."

"It does seem . . . a little suspicious," Toni added.

"I think it feels a *lot* suspicious," Cheryl clarified. "And I know just who the culprit is: those Baxter High Ravenettes."

"You know I'll murder them in cold blood if they're messing with you, babe," Toni said, "but why them? What makes you think they're behind this?"

"Um, how about the fact that their captain sent Cheryl out here?" I pointed out.

Betty considered it, too. "Well, obviously, that's suspect. But beyond that, what grudge would they have against us? Any more or worse than Stonewall, that is?"

Cheryl waved the dolls at us, their blank faces gazing numbly into the moonlight "Doesn't this just *scream* black magic to you?"

"It is . . . deeply *Blair Witch*–esque," I admitted, nodding.

"And if the pointed-toe witch's shoe fits . . ." Cheryl said, shaking the dolls again accusingly. "Everyone knows about the rumors that come out of Baxter High. Greendale is practically a hub of urban legendry! Who among us *hasn't* heard the tale of a paranormal phenomenon originating there?"

"Okay, fair," I said slowly, trying to keep Cheryl from going full force with her rising hysteria. "We've all heard the rumors." Witch trials and gruesome mass hangings, Satanic rituals, demonic possession . . . and those were just some of the more mundane anecdotes to come from that town. The world—at least the world that directly touched Riverdale—was divided into two camps of people: those who definitely didn't go trick-or-treating near Greendale . . . and those who *did*. And both for the same reasons. That said, I and my cohorts were of the persuasion that there was more than enough normal evil lurking in Riverdale without adding *para*normal into the mix.

"But you don't . . . actually *believe* in that stuff, right?" I looked from Cheryl to Betty to Toni, imploring them to see reason. I understood the impulse to leap to the most dramatic conclusion, but right now, thinking straight and keeping a clear head was feeling more urgent than ever.

"Normally I'd say no; I'm not easily swayed by tales of the mystic arts," Cheryl agreed. "But not believing that witchcraft is real is not the same as not believing that anyone would practice it. And what do these look like to you, if not some rudimentary form of voodoo dolls?"

"Maybe," Betty said. "But that doesn't necessarily mean Baxter High is behind it. It could just as easily mean that someone else wants us to *think* Baxter High is behind it. Or it could just be a random creepy coincidence." She reached for the dolls. "May I?"

Cheryl handed them to her, and Betty thoughtfully turned them over, examining them from every angle.

And then she did something extremely odd . . .

She *smiled*.

"Someone may or may not be targeting us, and we're alone out here in the woods, in the middle of a vicious storm," Toni said. "Why do you look so excited about it?"

"I think . . . well, these dolls may be a warning. But I think they also may be a clue. And now, I have a suspect or two in mind."

"That Lizzie girl? A fish rots from the head down, as the saying goes," Cheryl offered. "And her stunts were so subpar, I wouldn't blame her for being consumed by envy of our vastly superior skills. Maybe she's resorted to witchcraft in the hopes of improving her cheerleading."

"Just follow my lead," Betty said.

∧∧∧

Back in the mess hall, Betty swept to the center of the room, where the rest of the girls were eagerly awaiting us. "Relax," she said, holding up a hand before anyone could speak. "You guys were right. It was a mouse. That's why Cheryl was screaming."

Cheryl flashed Betty a look, obviously disappointed in that rather generic and lame cover story (knowing Cheryl, she would have wanted the fictional animal to have been something at least as big and intimidating as a bear), but she didn't protest. It turned out Betty knew what she was doing, and the prospect of a mouse was somehow concerning enough to turn most of the assembled girls off the whole game. I watched Stasia, Megan, Lizzie, and Jules as closely as I could, trying to pick up on any trace of suspicious behavior, but they looked exactly as confused-slash-apathetic as the rest of their squads did.

The thought that it might be a ruse in which they were *all* complicit flashed in my head, shades of the final scenes of *Rosemary's Baby*. One downside to my new life in Riverdale? It was getting harder and harder to tell when my horror movie–tinged hypotheses were running away with me.

"Game over on account of vermin, ladies," Cheryl said, adopting her signature stance of authority. "I've officially had my fill of 'funtivities' for the night. And I'll thank you to know that I'm *never* getting up close and personal with a pile of trash again in this lifetime—at least not willingly. I'm calling it: Vixens, we're going back to our bunk to try and finally relax."

"You're bailing on the dare, then? Just to be clear," Lizzie said.

Cheryl rolled her eyes. "Indeed. Feel free to call the eighth-grade police on me if you've got a problem with it." To the Vixens, she said, "Ladies, Ginger will lead you back to the cabin, and I'll be there shortly. Take care on the slippery paths!"

The girls all began to reassemble the dining hall into the arrangement it had been in when we arrived, slowly pulling on extra layers of clothing in preparation for the slog back to the cabins. To be honest, none of them looked disappointed to hear that our night was being cut short.

"Go on ahead, girls," Stasia said, waving to her own squad.

"I'm just going to grab some of those cookies I saw in the kitchen pantry. I'll be right up."

"We'll come with you," Betty said, loud. At Stasia's surprised look, she said, "I'm craving chocolate chip, what can I say?"

Of course, our girl had other things on her mind than cookies. Once the rest of the cheerleaders had dispersed (Ginger was only too pleased to take on the mantle of leading the Vixens back to the cabin as second-in-command, and the Ravenettes didn't linger, either), Toni, Betty, Cheryl, and I followed Stasia into the kitchen, stalking quickly and with purpose.

Stasia had opened the enormous, industrial-sized refrigerator and was taking a curious peek when Betty lurched forward and slammed it shut.

"What the hell?" Stasia asked, jumping back.

"It's cold in here," Betty said, glaring. "You were making it worse."

"If you're mad about that stupid 'truth' I answered, calm down," Stasia said. "I mean, your boy's definitely a cutie, and I'd be lying if I said I didn't wonder if he had a girlfriend when he first got to campus. But he made it abundantly clear that he did. So congrats, he's all yours. Not to mention, my family's straight off the Mayflower, and anyone I date seriously needs to be, too."

"How . . . charmingly ethnocentric," I said, arching an eyebrow.

Stasia shrugged, unbothered. "Sorry not sorry. The

scholarship kids are for fun, not for keeps. So if yours is taken? It's no big. I'm not out to, like, *steal* him or anything."

"Oh, phew," Betty snapped. "I was really worried."

"You can disperse with your feeble nonapologies, hag. Say what you will about Betty's admittedly low-rent beau, but that boy is nothing if not loyal," Cheryl put in. "I assure you, you couldn't get him to stray if you tried."

"That's—" Betty stepped forward, slightly flustered and wanting to get back on track. "Whatever. It's fine. I honestly don't care who you do or don't crush on, Stasia."

"Then what *do* you want?" she asked, coy. "Since the chocolate chip cookies are in that bin right there"—she pointed—"in plain sight. And this was obviously never about random late-night munchies."

Betty took a deep breath, clearly debating how best to approach the situation. In the end, she decided the direct approach was the way to go. "Why are you guys messing with us? The bed, the dumpsters . . . What are you up to?"

It was a calculated risk. Personally, I wasn't sure either of those incidents was specifically directed at us. But obvi, I'd have my girl's back during this interrogation, whatever the end result.

Stasia's eyes widened, and she laughed, a high, tinkling sound that dripped with scorn. "What are you even talking about?"

"The broken bunk bed," Betty said. "The one that ended up injuring me."

"I thought you said that wasn't serious," Stasia protested. "Now you think you were *targeted*?"

"I don't know *what* to think anymore," Betty said.

Stasia was nonchalant. "What else have you got? I mean, by way of actual proof, that is."

"It depends . . ." Betty said, reaching into her pocket. "What do you think of these?"

She held out the voodoo dolls, no less grotesque despite the fact that I knew what she was going to pull out even before she did it. Even without the element of surprise, these little beauties had the capacity to startle.

Stasia seemed to think so, too—she flinched. "Gross," she said dryly. "What *is* that?"

"You would know," Betty said. "You were the one who planted them in that dumpster for someone to find. My question is, why?"

"They look like little totems," Stasia offered, still skeptical. If she was posturing, she was doing an excellent job of it. Meryl Streep could have taken lessons from her in committing to a character. "I don't know why anyone would have them in the first place, except for some kind of spellcasting or something weird like that. Which—in case you haven't heard—is actually the Ravenettes' MO? Besides," she added, "if you found them in the dumpster, don't you think someone was probably throwing them away?"

"I just don't buy that it was totally coincidental," Betty said.

"Like I say, if they're voodoo dolls, then the obvious suspect is those Ravenettes," Stasia said, yawning.

"That's what we thought, at first," I chimed in. "It does make *some* sense. But Betty here has a real knack for getting to the bottom of tricky situations. And she had a feeling about you."

"The dolls' eyes were scribbled over with Sharpie," Betty said. "*Red* sharpie, to be specific. As you can plainly see. The same color Sharpie you were pocketing when we saw you in the infirmary earlier."

"You can't, like, *prove*—" Stasia started.

"Come on," Betty said. "Maybe it isn't the kind of evidence that would hold up in court, but coupled with your sketchy secret hideout in the infirmary bathroom, it's damning enough for now. And I'm *not* gonna let this go until you come clean."

"She's not exaggerating," I said, stepping forward. "You should know that Betty's the one who caught Jason Blossom's killer as well as the Sugarman *and* the Black Hood. Resistance is futile. You may as well tell us what you did and why."

Stasia looked off to one side for a moment, appearing to consider this. She glanced fleetingly at the kitchen door.

"Where are you gonna go?" Betty asked. "This camp's not that big. We've got the whole night ahead of us."

Stasia let out a huge sigh. "Fine, okay," she said. "But I think for the full story, we really are gonna need those cookies."

⌒⌒⌒

The rest of us weren't exactly craving a midnight snack (quasi-homicidal plots did little to stoke my appetite, personally), but we obliged Stasia and opened the box of cookies that Betty'd used as our original ruse for following Stasia to the kitchen in the first place. We watched her with growing impatience as she dunked one in a carton of milk and chewed it slowly, savoring.

"While we're young, please," Cheryl prompted her.

"You're right," Stasia said, looking Betty in the eye with some clear discomfort. "I mean, partially, anyway. Megan and I made those dolls. But I *didn't* put them in the dumpster or plan on you finding them. I don't know how they got there. They were supposed to be for the Ravenettes . . . but I had changed my mind."

"And my bed?" Betty demanded.

Stasia shook her head. "Not me. I swear. I assume it was just an accident."

"Except that literally nothing about this weekend so far is feeling accidental," I muttered, mostly to myself.

"You made those voodoo dolls. For the Ravenettes," Betty continued. "And you and Lizzie were both completely weird and evasive about why your squads stopped coming to Sweetwater Pines for your annual retreat. Why? What are you not telling us?"

"It's . . ." Stasia took a deep breath. "There's this thing. This history at Stonewall. I don't know, maybe Jughead mentioned it to you?"

We all glanced at Betty, who shook her head.

Stasia swallowed. "Some people say it's a curse." She looked embarrassed.

"Your school is cursed?" Betty echoed, dubious.

"I mean, call it what you want," Stasia said, "but—you guys must have heard of the Stonewall Four?"

"The only thing I know about your second-rate prep school is that it apparently isn't all that elite, given Jughead Jones is your newest student," Cheryl spat.

"Cheryl," Betty snapped. And then: "Is this curse what Lizzie was talking about? Missing students?"

"Yeah." Stasia nodded. "Every decade or so, someone goes missing. Four in total—so far. The administration tries to keep it on the DL—wouldn't want the school's pristine reputation getting tarnished. And, since the students are missing and not . . . well, not officially dead . . . well, it's easier to keep the media at bay."

"It's amazing what money and a little bit of clout can get you." I folded my arms over my chest. "Trust me, I know from personal experience."

"Okay, but what does all this have to do with you terrorizing the Baxter High girls, here and now?" Betty asked. "Do you think *Baxter* has something to do with the Stonewall Four?"

"I don't know," Stasia said. "Those disappearances happened over, like, forty years; they might be totally unconnected. But . . . there was another incident."

"The one you and Lizzie were both dancing around during truth or dare," Cheryl said.

"Maybe you guys haven't heard about it, but the Ravenettes are notorious for hazing," Stasia said. "There's a reason it took Lizzie, like, a split second to come up with that dumpster dare—that was nothing for her. I mean, there are urban legends about some of the stuff they've pulled—at cheer retreats right at this very camp!"

"Will wonders never cease?" Cheryl mused. "So, for once, Brigitte Reilly wasn't just babbling on about nothing. She was talking all about that when we first arrived. Some silly campfire story about a girl who was hazed to death."

"It wasn't silly. One of our old squad members, Judy Johnson, she was a scholarship student, too, and she was really self-conscious about it."

"It probably doesn't help that you guys are always harping on things like class and money, from what it sounds like," Toni said.

Stasia shook her head. "I mean, I was only a freshman, so I can't even say what really happened. But she went missing—on one of these very retreats." She looked down. "That may be the source of your so-called campfire story."

Toni's eyes flew open. "Someone went *missing* on a cheer retreat? *Here?* And this place is still open for business?" She shook her head and reached for a cookie from the box. "Real talk: Again I ask, *what the hell* is everyone around here smoking?" She looked at Cheryl. "I cannot tell you how much I can't wait to graduate and flee this Bermuda Triangle of mysterious disasters forever."

"You know I love your flights of fancy, and I'd be thrilled to speculate about our limitless future," Cheryl said, planting a kiss on Toni's cheek, "but perhaps we should focus right now, as it seems like our personal well-being may depend on it."

"So Judy went missing," Stasia went on, "and . . . well, that was that."

"You don't know what happened to her?"

"Hence 'missing,'" Stasia said, waving her hand. "After she vanished one night during a retreat, her parents put out a search party. But after a few weeks of no leads . . . well, the trail went cold. She was presumed dead. That was all anyone would say. But there were rumors. That there had been hazing, that something went wrong and she was hurt—maybe even *killed*. And I *know* it wasn't at the hands of our squad. There's no way."

"Meaning it had to be the Ravenettes," Betty said.

"Exactly," Stasia said. "You know, we almost weren't going to come this weekend. When we got that invitation, people were . . . well, no one was eager to reopen old wounds. But then we heard that the Baxter High squad was planning to be here, too. So, we thought . . ."

"You thought you'd come to the retreat and mess with them. Maybe give them a little well-earned payback for hazing your former teammate? And, if you were lucky, fill in some of the blanks surrounding Judy's disappearance, too?"

"I didn't mean to get you guys involved," Stasia said. "I—we—were going to leave those dolls in the Baxter cabin, just to creep them out. But I don't know—when it came time to plant them, it felt petty, so I called it off. I'm telling you, I have no idea how they ended up in the dumpster. Maybe one of the other Queens was trying to do me a favor? I told Megan to get rid of them, so . . . maybe that's how she decided to do it? I swear, I never expected you guys to find them.

"I *am* sorry you guys got caught in the crossfire," Stasia continued. "And maybe I shouldn't have been plotting against the Ravenettes in the first place. But . . . they're connected to what happened to Judy. I just know it. They *have* to be." She looked at us, eyes shiny. "Because if they're not, then we have no leads at all."

I softened toward her. I knew what it was like, to be embroiled in something sinister, something violent, and not know which way to turn. We all did. Toni, Betty, Cheryl, and I seemed to reach the same conclusion at the same time, each grabbing one another's hands until we were forming a protective circle of sorts with Stasia.

"Well, an urban legend and some school-wide rumors don't give us a lot of proof that the Ravenettes had anything to do with what happened to your former squad mate," Betty started. "But something weird is definitely going on here. And it just so happens that I'm *excellent* at finding leads. Everything Veronica said about me solving mysteries? One hundred percent true. So, if you want my help keeping an eye on the Ravenettes, I'm in." She glanced at each of us, and we each gave a short nod back.

"We're all in."

CHAPTER SEVENTEEN

Jughead:

JB, how're you holding up? Power's been going on and off at La Bonne Nuit. Tell me you're staying inside and staying safe . . .

Jughead:

Text me back, even if you're still mad I sent you home, OK?

Jughead:

You can be angry, but humor me anyway.

JB:

I'm fine. But I AM angry.

Jughead:

I'm OK with that.

JB:

🙏 ☺

∿∿∿

ARCHIE

"Dodger? What the hell is going on here? How'd you guys even get in here?"

Dodger was basically a street thug who'd recently made it his life's mission to mess with the kids who hung at the community center. I couldn't believe he'd managed to track me down here and now, of all times and places. But then again, he did have a habit of showing up when I least expected it—and when I least wanted to see him.

"We have our ways," he said, smiling at me. He and the rest of his crew started to make their way into the speakeasy proper, grinning and surveying the place.

"Nice setup for your little poker night. We were angling for an invitation, but I guess you lost my number."

"Yeah, well," I said, still struggling to follow what was going on, "we were trying to keep the guest list closed off to people who've, you know, threatened me and my community center kids."

The pot was still missing, and now there were people here I hadn't even known about. What about that crack security system Reggie had been going on about? *Whole lot of good it was doing us right now.* Dodger and his team were straight-up *dangerous*, and I knew that they could cause serious trouble if that's what they wanted to do.

I felt beads of sweat prick up all over my body: The more

people that were in here, the more places where that money could be—and the harder it would be to track down. Not to mention, there was no way Dodger was just here to make nice.

"Look, guys, whatever you were planning, just forget it," I said. "There's money missing—a lot of it. And we have to figure out where it went. And with you all just showing up right now, I have to say, you're prime suspects. My boys aren't afraid to take you, if that's what it comes to." I nodded to Munroe and Reggie, who both stepped closer, puffing their chests up.

Dodger smirked. "Oh, man. *Please*—let's get into it. I'm just dying to have a real go at you." He spread his arms out, indicating his whole crew. "We all are."

I looked around the room, considering. Everyone was tense, worried. Kevin was clutching Frankie's arm, and even Peaches, usually so tough, was bouncing on her toes, radiating nervous energy. The money was missing. And now it turns out we weren't only locked downstairs, but we were locked downstairs with a legit psychopath who had violent tendencies.

Enough was enough. I pulled out my cell. "I'm calling the cops. You guys aren't gonna give us any trouble. So get ready to get gone—and leave the money you stole behind."

"Except, counterpoint, Archie," Kevin said, eager and nervous at the bar. "You're running an illegal gambling night with multiple games where alcohol is being served to minors. I can't say that calling the police feels like the *best* idea."

"He's right, Arch," Jughead said. "Maybe that can be our plan B?"

I fumed. They were right, of course.

The problem was, we didn't have a viable plan *A*.

CHAPTER EIGHTEEN

BETTY

I woke with a start, my body slick with sweat, heart pounding.
I must have been dreaming—something about hazy, ominous,
gauzy white figures darting through the woods. When we
finally returned to our cabin after our confrontation with
Stasia, no one was really all that eager to get to bed. It was
unsettling, going to sleep with Coach Grappler still out there,
god knew where, (hopefully) still dealing with the broken-
down bus. But in the end, we were exhausted, and there wasn't
much else to do about Coach Grappler until the storm died
down and we could get a cell signal, anyway. So even though
sleep had been the farthest thing from my mind, I had still
managed to drift off. But what had woken me?

As the haze of sleep began to wash away and consciousness
slowly crept back over me, I realized what it was: a banging
sound—sharp, insistent, steady—coming from outside.

A banging, and a steady wail.

I peeled back the covers from my bed—I'd reluctantly taken
over Coach Grappler's when it became clear she wasn't going
to show tonight and my bunk proved irreparable—and stepped

cautiously onto the wood-planked floor, the grain cold and fine under my toes.

From the corner of my eye, I saw a flicker—something white and diaphanous skating past our window. Something like what I kept imagining I saw in the woods? Like what I saw in my dream?

"Betty?" Veronica sat up, switching on a flashlight. "What are you doing?"

I held a finger up, *shh*, and jerked my head toward the window. "There's something out there. Running around."

Veronica's eyes narrowed. "Did it wake anyone else?"

I shook my head, casting a quick glance around the room. Everyone was still sleeping peacefully it seemed like. Nancy Woods had fallen asleep with a copy of *The Goldfinch* tucked under one arm—it was a brick; she'd probably have a cramp in that arm when she finally woke up—and Toni had, unsurprisingly, gone against her original threat to Cheryl and fallen asleep in Cheryl's tiny bed with her, the two curled up around each other like a matching set. "Not yet."

I started to step into my boots and pulled a windbreaker on over my pj's, not thinking beyond getting outside and getting to the bottom of this, once and for all. Veronica watched me for a second before she got up and followed suit.

"I would like to go on record saying that only for you, Betty Cooper, would I willingly go out in a driving storm to investigate a strange noise at a creepy sleepaway camp." She sighed.

"I mean, this is ripped straight from the pages of an old Christopher Pike novel, right?"

I shrugged. "We'll know soon enough."

Quietly, we crept toward the door.

Outside, there was no sign of the white flash I'd seen darting past the window. Instead, I immediately saw the source of the banging sound: It was the Baxter High cabin door, blowing open and closed again in the blustery wind.

"Why wouldn't they have latched that?" Veronica asked, voicing my exact thoughts.

I didn't have a chance to offer an opinion before the girls themselves came streaking toward us, shrieking. This wasn't the wailing I'd heard when I woke from my nightmare—this was something worse, something primal and filled with terror.

"What is the meaning of this?"

It was Cheryl, covered dramatically in a shiny red poncho, looking for all the world like a Disney character lost in the woods. Toni was at her side, also in the thermals she'd slept in with a pair of rain boots and a thin nylon hooded top. Both were wide-eyed, taking in the scene. Around us, the Baxter High girls were racing, frantic, babbling incoherently. In the distance, their door continued to clap open and closed. One by one, the Vixens wandered outside, groggy, curious, tentative, investigating with caution and fear.

"I have no idea," I confessed.

The door to the Ravenettes' cabin flew open again, and this time, a series of what I could only describe as creatures came rushing out, ghostly, pale wings outspread, hooting in unnerving, guttural calls. Whatever these . . . things were, they were . . .

"They're *chasing* the Ravenettes," I said, realizing. "Down . . . to the waterfront?"

"Who is it, though?" Veronica asked. "They look like refugees from a Guillermo del Toro movie."

"Only one way to find out," I said. We all exchanged a glance.

We didn't have time to speculate, or think. Instead, the four of us took off after the shapes, after the Ravenettes, into the darkness and the swirling storm. We ran toward the center of the camp, its murky, beating heart: the lake.

∧∧∧

The path was muddy as ever, and we struggled to keep up with the figures moving in the distance. Toni slipped once, sliding down along one hip, and we all stopped briefly to help her back to her feet. By the time we got down to the waterfront, we were all streaked with mud and grime, our boots heavy with it.

"What . . . *is* it?" Cheryl asked. We all stopped, breathing hard, and looked where she was looking, down toward the water's edge.

There, silhouetted in the moonlight, were the Ravenettes, all on their knees, some sobbing, some keening, some calling out in fear. Hovering over them were . . .

I moved closer. "They're *costumes*. Halloween costumes. Like you'd get at the dollar store. Ghosts, I guess."

"So it's a Wes Craven movie," Veronica said. "I stand corrected. But *why*?"

I stomped forward and yanked the glorified bedsheet off one figure. It was Stasia. "What the hell?" I got close to her, peering directly into her eyes. "You said you only wanted to keep an eye on the Ravenettes."

"No one is getting hurt," Stasia said innocently. One by one the girls removed their costumes. "It's just a stupid prank."

"We told you we'd help you investigate the Baxter High cheerleaders," I said. "But you promised the hazing was over, that it was just those creepy dolls. So what the hell is going on, Stasia?"

Slowly the Ravenettes stood, gathering themselves. "Investigating us?" Lizzie demanded. "For what? And how is it *your* business, anyway, Sandra Dee?"

"All this hazing stuff, it started with *your* school!" I said. "And now we find out it might be connected to a missing student . . . at the school my boyfriend *just* transferred to. You'd better believe this is my business."

"And we will definitely sort it all out," said a small voice. I turned to see one of the quieter Ravenettes, eyes wide, chin trembling, gazing out at the waterfront. "But, like—what's your friend doing out there on the lake?"

It was hard to tell, between the darkness and the rain and the general confusion. But it looked as though Cheryl had wandered out to the small dock, leaning off the edge, her red slicker flashing like a warning sign as lightning darted overhead.

"Cheryl, what are you doing?" Toni called, cupping her hands at her mouth to be heard over the storm. "That doesn't look safe in this weather!" She moved to follow her girlfriend, and I jumped in line behind her. It *didn't* look safe, but maybe there was strength in numbers.

At the dock, Cheryl twisted to see us. She raised an arm, waving toward something. Was that—did I see that streak of something, again? I flashed back to those moments in the woods, first walking to camp from the bus, and then for a sec- ond time on the way to the infirmary with Veronica, that split second when I'd thought, for a beat, that the forest was alive around me.

If it was there, it was gone just as quickly as I'd registered it in the first place.

But there were too many bodies, too much happening right now. My own mind was coming unwound, becoming unreliable.

"Compatriots!" Cheryl called, straining to be heard. "I think I see—"

I heard a *splash*.

It happened in the blink of an eye, literally. One second, Cheryl was there, red hood gleaming in the glow of the night storm, rain sluicing down the outline of her body against the sky. The next, there was a splash, and a ripple in the water, and nothing but a stray corner of red vinyl, bobbing at the surface of the water.

"*Cheryl!*" Toni screamed, taking off to the end of the dock, full force, after her.

But Cheryl was gone.

PART THREE:
SECRETS AND SINS

CHAPTER NINETEEN

REGGIE

"Sit and stay," I said, looming over Dodger and his boys.

"Watch that tone," he said, glaring at me, but he didn't get up.

We'd forced the intruders into seats, and the Serpents and Poisons were both watching over them, keeping them in their places while we searched the speakeasy for the missing money. I had a lot on the line here—not just the missing pot itself, but the fact that everyone thought *I'd* taken it.

"This place used to have a fallout shelter," I said. I moved to the back of the speakeasy, sliding a large maple barrel that was propped against the wall out of the way. Once I did, we could all clearly see the outline of a waist-high opening in the paneling. "We use it for overflow storage now, but it's solid as a rock. With just a few key places where someone shady like you"—I shot a look at Dodger—"could hide a stash of stolen money."

"Maybe it's less solid than you thought," Dodger said.

"Yeah," Jughead said, stepping forward and crouching to peek inside, his arm outstretched and his phone flashlight on. "Maybe so." His voice echoed from inside the tiny room.

"What's in there?" Archie called out.

Jughead stepped out, adjusting his beanie. "Honestly, nothing. Dust. A few old crates that must've held some liquor bottles, once upon a time. It's just a storage closet. But if the money's in there, it's invisible."

"I told you, we didn't take your damn money. We were just trying to have a little fun," Dodger said, leering. "Looks like we got our wish."

Archie stepped closer to him, his face stern. "Just because we're not calling the cops on you—*yet*—doesn't mean we couldn't take you if we tried."

"Uh, maybe let's put a pin in that," Munroe called, sounding nervous. "I found something—*someone*—else. In the bathroom."

We all turned to see Munroe with a newcomer—the last person we expected to find here.

Jughead's jaw practically hit the floor. "JB? What are you—? I told you to—! We were literally *just* texting!"

"She was hiding in one of the stalls," Munroe said, looking equal parts proud and sorry to have to report the news.

JB blushed. "Sorry."

"That's—that's not good enough!" Jughead sputtered. "I told you to go home."

"And *I* told you I was a big girl." She put her hands on her hips, defiant. "Besides," she added, "you actually need me right now."

"What are you talking about?" Jughead asked.

"The cameras are down, right?" she said, smirking. "I've got a backup. I set up my own phone to record the game through a hole in the wall of the bathroom."

Jughead looked stunned. "That's . . . well, it's incredibly creepy, and probably illegal."

JB looked uneasy, but she summoned up some swagger. "I told you, I'm practically a Serpent. I thought maybe if I could get an extra camera on your poker night, I'd be doing you a favor. Insurance, or whatever. *Like in case someone tried to pull something.*" She glared at me.

"And *I* told you, you're *not* a Serpent. Not yet, anyway. Protecting you is one of the few ways I can take care of you with Mom gone. And regardless of your intentions, planting surveillance behind everyone's back is pretty damn shady." Jughead shook his head. "But it actually turns out, it's also pretty damn helpful right now." He narrowed his eyes. "Consider it a lucky break, not a reprieve."

JB just nodded.

And speaking of reprieves . . . My heart jumped into my throat. How could I keep everyone from looking at the footage?

Before I had a chance to try anything, JB had grabbed her phone and brought it to Jughead. Archie and Munroe leaped to his side to examine what she'd captured.

Crap. This was it. The whole thing, all my hard work— done. Poof.

Because I knew what the three of them were looking at. Not me pocketing the pot, because I actually *hadn't* done that.

But I *had* tampered with the poker deck to deal myself winning hand after winning hand.

Archie looked up, red in the face. Clearly, he'd just gotten to the grand finale of JB's little home video. He took a deep breath and lunged for me, furious, but Munroe held him back. "Are you freaking kidding with this?"

"What the *hell*, man?" Jughead shouted, as murmurs of outrage washed over the room. From his seat by the bar, Dodger just cackled at the mess unraveling before his eyes.

"Wait, let me explain!" I held my hands up, protesting. "I *was* cheating. That's why I was winning so big. I'm sorry, man. It was a crappy thing to do, I admit it. But I *didn't* steal the pot, I swear."

Jughead held his hands up like he was weighing something. "I mean . . . you were going to, though. If you were winning via cheating. How is that any different?"

"Maybe it's not, man! I told you, I know it was wrong," I said, exasperated. "I just needed the money." I looked away. "I'm . . . well, I'm trying to save up enough so I can move out of my house."

No one had anything to say to that. I knew most of them understood why I was looking to relocate. It was humiliating . . . but I guess it was better than being crucified for stealing something I'd never actually stolen. "I'm just saying—I've got nothing to do with the missing money *now* . . . I just . . . messed with the deck. When I was shuffling. I don't know what happened to the pot, though, honestly."

"Twist," Kevin breathed, grabbing Frankie's arm. "This is so much better than any CW soap." But Archie and Jughead just rolled their eyes; I could tell they weren't totally buying my story.

"You don't believe me?" I asked them, the panic of a few minutes ago fading away. "Fine, I'll prove I didn't do this."

I clapped and then turned to face the rest of the room. "Listen up!" I said, mustering every ounce of Big Bulldog Energy I could summon. "I don't care who's down here or who was hiding where when. Yeah, I messed with the cards. But that's not the issue right now."

"I mean, it's *a little bit* of the issue, maybe?" Sweet Pea said, arching an eyebrow at me.

"Great. Whatever. You guys can tar and feather me *later*. But first things first: There's money missing. A crap load of it. And we're gonna find it."

"Not if we find it first," Dodger said, voice low.

"Look around, dude," I said, sweeping my arms out at my sides. "Think about what Archie said. There's more than enough of us to take you guys."

Dodger glanced at one of his stooges, a greasy-haired guy with a face full of acne scars. The two began to cackle. "The thing is, *dude*," Dodger said, "*we* brought reinforcements."

Lightning-quick, he whipped something small and silver out of his pocket. It glinted in the low light of the speakeasy. Then he pressed a button and with a soft *click*, a blade emerged, and we realized just what he meant by "reinforcements."

"Bro," Archie said to me, as though we weren't all looking at the exact same thing. "He's got a knife."

"I see it," I said, breathing hard.

I just wasn't sure what we should—what we *could*—do about it.

CHAPTER TWENTY

VERONICA

The rain was everywhere—in my clothes, my boots, my eyes—so heavy that the entire surreal scene unfolding around me felt all the more otherworldly. One minute Cheryl was *right there*, standing on the dock, calling to us. The next, she was gone, her raincoat bobbing at the surface of the lake like a bloodstain, loud and accusing.

In a flash, Toni had jumped in after her.

"We have to—call someone!" Betty cried, running up beside me.

"Who, though? No one's getting service."

Betty grabbed me, her eyes bright with realization—and also fear. "The main office. There was a phone in there. On the desk. A landline—old-school. We could call nine-one-one."

"I've got her!" It was Toni, waterlogged and gasping. She reached one arm up, flailing. With the other, she cradled an unconscious Cheryl above the surface of the lake. "She's got a pulse, but I don't think she's breathing!"

Betty dropped to her stomach. She snaked her arms over

the dock and under Cheryl's shoulders. "I can take her. Are you okay to get up yourself?"

"I've got it," I said. I beckoned to Toni, who paddled my way, and held out an arm to steady her as she hoisted herself onto the dock.

We both turned, bedraggled and wet, to see Betty laying Cheryl down on the dock. By the moonlight, her typically alabaster skin looked ghostly pale.

"Is she okay?" It was Stasia, leaning over us with worry in her eyes.

Betty put her head to Cheryl's mouth. "I know CPR."

"Are you . . . ? What should I . . ." Stasia seemed truly overwhelmed by the situation, but her emotional state was the last thing we had time for right now.

"Listen," Betty said, forceful. "I'm going to do the CPR. She's going to be fine, I promise. But—I swear, I thought I saw something out in the woods. And that means . . ."

"It means, maybe Cheryl didn't just *slip* into the water," Toni said, realizing.

"Exactly," Betty said, grim. "So can you go—*run*—to the main office and call for help? Whatever's going on here, I think it's bigger than some random hazing pranks, and I definitely think we could be in real danger."

Stasia's eyes went wide. "I can do it, of course."

"Good," I said. "Then go."

She ran off, beckoning to her friends to follow her. Around

us, the Baxter High girls had dispersed, too, though what came next on this night of horrors was a total question mark to me. But again—I didn't have time to worry about that right now. Betty was on the ground, pounding rhythmically on Cheryl's chest and pausing intermittently to breathe into her mouth.

"Come on, babe," Toni pleaded, taking one of Cheryl's limp hands in her own.

Suddenly, Betty pulled back. Cheryl shuddered, then turned her head to one side and coughed up a great gush of water. She slowly sat up. "What . . . happened?"

Toni threw her arms around her in exuberant relief. "You fell into the water," she said. "I was so worried, babe. But Betty brought you back."

"*You* brought me back," Cheryl said, gazing at Toni with adoration. "You pulled me out of the raging waters—that much I was vaguely conscious for. My heroine." She kissed Toni. "And, of course, I'm grateful to you, too, Betty." She looked down, slightly abashed. "You and your chums are responsible for saving me from a watery grave twice over now."

"We're just *so* relieved you're okay," I said. "But, Cheryl— what happened? Did you slip? Or—" I thought of what Betty said—how she thought she'd seen something moving in the distance—and shivered.

Cheryl made an indignant face. "Of course not. You know my coordination is unparalleled." She narrowed her gaze, her eyebrows pulled tight. "I didn't slip. I was pushed."

"Oh my god," I said, my worst fears confirmed. "By *who*? I mean, we were standing right with all the Baxter and Stonewall girls, and we didn't see anyone over by the dock."

Cheryl shuddered. "I don't know. But there was something moving . . . out here, by the lake. Everyone was so ensconced in the fray, no one was paying attention. So I ventured out to investigate it myself. And when I got to the edge of the dock, something, or some*one*—jumped out—from the woods? I don't know, it happened so fast. But it—they—came out of nowhere, and they pushed me. And I went under."

I glanced around, seeing nothing but sheets of rain and tall stalks of tree branches waving in the distance. "This thing, or person, or whatever . . . what did it look like?"

"Like a flash of . . . white. Floating," Betty said, cutting in. Her eyes glittered with dark knowledge.

"Exactly," Cheryl said, looking at Betty curiously. "How did you know, cousin?"

"Because I've seen it myself," Betty said simply. "Earlier. A couple of times. "

"Why didn't you say anything?" I asked, surprised.

She sighed. "I . . . honestly didn't trust my own eyes. So I wanted to hold out until I was sure. And now I am." She fixed her gaze at a point on the horizon, where the path from the waterfront led back into the dark, twisting woods. "Because it's right there." She pointed toward that path, beckoning like an open mouth. "Whatever, whoever, the hell it was, it just ran into the forest."

She stood up.

"And I'm going after it."

I ran after Betty, without hesitation, into the forest, leaving Toni and Cheryl in our wake. The woods were alive now, sentient with the scents and sounds of the storm—twigs crackling beneath our feet, low-hanging branches slapping our faces as we streaked through the night. I *hadn't* seen whatever it was that Betty saw—and in truth, I was somewhat grateful for that, given the things I *had* seen since we'd first left on this ill-fated trip—but I didn't doubt her, or her sense that we were in peril.

We ran, pushing uphill, barely able to see more than a few inches in front of our faces. I was so thoroughly soaked I felt it in my skin, my pores, my bones, and every stray sound set the hairs on the back of my neck on edge.

Then there was a sound that gutted me to the core.

It was Betty, screaming, sharp and bright, scrambling back, clutching me.

"What?" I asked, my heart pounding in my throat, my eyes darting suspiciously from dark corner to dark corner.

In answer, she sobbed, and pulled me closer to her. She tilted my chin, pointed me in the direction of where she'd been looking.

It was Coach Grappler. Tied to a tree. She was gagged . . . And her eyes.

Her eyes.

Someone had gouged out her eyes. They trailed red, sockets empty and unseeing, reminding me briefly of those lurid little dolls the Queens had concocted to frighten the Ravenettes.

But this wasn't a doll, and it wasn't Sharpie. This was real-life, our coach, bound and strung like a hunting trophy.

"Coach," Betty moaned.

I turned to one side and retched, my stomach heaving until there was nothing left inside to bring up.

"Betty," I said, "we have to get to the main office. Stasia must have called nine-one-one by now. I don't know what's going on, but I'm thinking it's our only—"

I didn't have a chance to finish that sentence, though, before everything went black.

CHAPTER TWENTY-ONE

Operator: Nine-one-one, what is your emergency?

Caller: We're at the camp. Someone is—oh god!

Operator: Which camp, sweetheart? Can you just give me the name?

Caller: There's someone after us!

Operator: Are you currently in danger?

Caller: Yes! *Yes!* Someone is *trying to kill us here.* Please send help. Camp Sweet—

Operator: Caller, are you there?

Operator: Caller, are you still with me?

CALL FAILED

∧∧∧

Jughead:

> Dad, we've got a situation at the speakeasy. Can you come?

FP Jones:

Boy, what have you been up to?

Jughead:

Some decidedly PG-13 stuff, I admit. But we need you.

Jughead:

Things are getting serious.

FP Jones:

Are you in physical danger?

Jughead:

Not yet. But . . .

Jughead:

Well, it's better if you get here—quick.

Jughead:

JB's here. She's OK, but . . .

FP Jones:

I'm on my way.

Jughead:

I never thought I'd say this, but I'm kind of missing your peppy emoji signoffs.

FP Jones:

What are you talking about? Did you lose your mind down in that speakeasy, along with whatever else?

Jughead:

When you were texting me about JB yesterday, you were using all those emojis . . . ?

Jughead:

Wait . . .

Jughead:

Never mind. I need to think. But I'll see you soon.

⌒⌒⌒

JUGHEAD

I pulled JB over toward the storage room, needing a moment alone with her. (Or as alone as we could get locked into an underground speakeasy with half of Riverdale High.) "Level with me," I said, serious. "Is there another entrance into the speakeasy?"

The Serpents and the Poisons had finally managed to put aside whatever tension they were still nursing to surround

Dodger together, restraining him, so for the time being, his knife was a nonissue. His crew had wisely chosen to stand down, seeing as how their five thugs were easily outnumbered by us, weapons or no. But I still wouldn't exhale until my dad arrived. In the meantime, though, I was having what could only be described as a bona fide hunch.

She shook her head. "Don't you think Reggie would have told you about it if there was?"

"In case you haven't noticed, tonight hasn't been great for Reggie's credibility. And I'm not convinced that you managed to sneak in down the stairs, right past me, blackout or no. So I'm wondering how else you might have gotten in here."

"I mean, you searched this place yourself, right?" She peered at me, intense. "You didn't find anything."

"I didn't," I agreed. "But I'm working on a new theory."

"What?" JB asked, wary.

"Yesterday I got a text from Dad," I said to her, speaking deliberately. "Funny enough, he signed off using a bunch of emojis—which you have to admit is pretty out of character."

"I mean, what can I say, I guess I'm rubbing off on the old man." She looked doubtful.

"Yeah. But whenever I've mentioned it since then, he's had no idea what I'm talking about," I said. "Hence, my theory."

Her eyes darted around the room. I could tell she was struggling to maintain her composure.

I scrolled through my phone's call log. When I got to the text Dad had sent yesterday, I hit CALL BACK.

"I thought no one was getting any service," JB said in an unnaturally high voice.

I showed her my screen. "One bar," I said. "I think it'll be enough."

"Enough for *what*?" she squeaked.

I held up a finger and *shushed* her. "Wait for it . . ."

One second.

Two.

Three.

There.

Coming from the storage room, I heard it: the distinct electronic chime of a cell phone.

I grabbed JB by the arm and pulled her inside. "Do you have something to tell me?" I shone my flashlight into a corner onto a stack of crates.

"Jughead, you're being super weird," she said. But her eyes darted everywhere *but* my own gaze, so I knew I was on to something.

"Why don't you slide those crates out of the way," I suggested.

She cast me another dubious look, then did as I said.

"Look at that!" I said, all fake chipper.

Her mouth dropped open. She looked genuinely stunned. "I . . . don't," she said. "I mean, *I* had no idea that was there."

In the wall, behind where the crates had been stacked, there was a rectangular groove in the stone face. I pushed it—and a large square sheet of stone slid inward, revealing a deep hole within the storage room.

And *in* that hole?

Was a cell phone.

The phone didn't surprise me. What *did* surprise me was JB's friend Ricky, hunched on the floor beside it, looking totally busted.

I grabbed him by the collar and dragged him out to the center of the speakeasy. Everyone in the room was shocked. Kevin gasped like he was auditioning for a soap opera, and Archie leaped toward us, baffled and angry.

"What the *hell*, man? Where did he even come from?" he asked.

"Partners in crime," I said, gesturing to Ricky and JB in one swoop of my arm, though it was mainly rhetorical.

Ricky nodded. "We're with the Serpents."

"Like *hell* you are," Sweet Pea said, coming up behind me. "The last thing we need is Joaquin's kid brother's blood on our hands because we brought him into the gang life before he was even out of middle school."

"First thing we've agreed on all night, man," Peaches said, jumping into the conversation. "JB, you know I'm around for you. But here? This is no place for you. Not yet."

"I—I don't . . ." JB faltered.

"Wait, wait! JB's friend Ricky is *Ricky DeSantos*?" Archie asked, suddenly at my side. "How am I just putting this together?"

"It's been a big night," Kevin put in kindly.

"I can't believe you'd show your face here, man," Archie said, glaring at Ricky. "You conned me, and Veronica. And then you *stabbed me*. And now you're hanging out with Jughead's sister?"

Ricky went pale. "I—I didn't mean to."

Archie's eyebrows flew up. "You didn't *mean* to?"

"I didn't want to," he protested. His voice shook slightly. "It was a quest. They said I had to. To avenge Joaquin and finish the game."

"It was G and G," I said, stepping in, "and while he *did* stab you, Archie, I can vouch for Ricky. Let's just say your previous interactions were out of character."

Archie threw some major side eye at JB and Ricky. "But apparently it's *in* character for him to be hiding out in La Bonne Nuit during a lockdown? Cool."

I shook my head, eager to get back on track. "JB, why don't you go and grab that phone in there," I said, nodding back toward the storage closet. "I'll bet you the stolen money that it's going to show a missed call from me."

"You're, um, making a lot of assumptions," JB said, her voice quavering ever so slightly.

I looked at Ricky. "How long have you been down here?"

He shrugged. "Long enough. The game was open to Serpents, wasn't it?"

"Again, you're not a Serpent," Peaches said to Ricky. "Neither of you is. And you're not a Poison yet, either, JB." She turned to me. "JB's been hanging around, wanting to get in on our action, but I keep telling her not yet." She leveled me with a serious gaze. "Might be that she's missing having someone around, looking after her, more regularly. Though I'm guessing she won't admit it."

"There's nothing to admit!" JB blurted. "And by the way, this place wasn't a *fallout shelter*, it was a speakeasy originally. That's the whole reason Veronica had the idea to turn it *back* into a speakeasy after she bought Pop's."

"And since a place like that would have been in major demand during Prohibition, it makes sense that there was a secret exit *someplace* so that imbibers could make a quick getaway in case of a raid," I added, still piecing things together myself. I paused and turned to look at my kid sister. "Or so teenage troublemakers could sneak *in* to an off-limits poker game, disable a smart security system, and steal the pot."

JB looked at me, holding my gaze.

After a beat, a wide smile split her face. "Well done, big bro!" She laughed. "Bet you didn't think I had it in me."

"Fomenting chaos? I definitely knew you had *that* in you. What I *didn't* know was that you've become a skilled techno thief. I'm impressed that you managed to out the power for the whole building, JB."

"That wasn't me," she said. "That was the actual storm. I just used the blackout as an opportunity to grab the money and reroute the security system to the burner phone. But then, when I went back to grab *my* phone from where it was recording in the bathroom, the power had come back on and everyone was freaking out, so I was stuck in there."

"And you couldn't get back to Ricky, who had the money," I filled in. "I have to admit, it's clever," I said. "But you're still in major trouble. And you're going to have to try harder to sound like Dad the next time you want to *convince me* that you're Dad."

I sighed then, softening. "What's going on with you, JB?" I asked. "Since when are you a thief?"

"I'm not a *thief*," she sniffed.

"Then what do you call this *Ocean's Eleven* poker heist you just pulled off? And what's *this*?" I reached out and grabbed for the slim, delicate chain around her neck. She'd tucked it under her shirt, but I'd seen the telltale clasp peeking out at the nape of her neck, where her braids fanned off into opposite directions.

It was an antique cameo. And it was Betty's.

JB met my gaze, unflinching. "I know what you're thinking," she said. "But she gave it to me."

"And I know you're lying, JB," I said softly. "Because Betty got that necklace from Polly. And as much as she adores you, she'd never, ever give it up."

"Fine." JB folded her arms over her chest. "You think you're so smart. You don't even know the half of what we've been up to." She gave a smug look to Ricky, who returned it.

Realization dawned, hitting me like a full maple barrel. "You and Ricky have been behind all the petty vandalism and the little crimes going on around town?"

"Guess you're not *such* a brilliant detective," she snapped. "Took you long enough to put that together."

"But . . . *why*, JB?" I asked. "I mean, if you wanted money, I'm sure Veronica could hook you up making deliveries for Pop on your bike or something."

"I don't need money," she sneered. "I just wanted . . . I don't know. I wanted to do something exciting." She stared at me, her gaze piercing. "Mom's gone. Dad's busy. You're off at your fancy new school. I thought maybe . . . if I got the money from poker night for Peaches, she'd . . . I don't know. She'd make me a Poison now instead of forcing me to wait to be a Serpent, like you."

I turned to Peaches, horrified. "Did you know she was doing all this?"

"I didn't know the extent of it," Peaches said. "But I knew she was having a tough time."

"And you didn't think to mention it to me?" I asked.

"You've been away, man," Peaches pointed out. "You

say you're here for everyone—for your gang, for your family—but you're not *actually* here."

I sighed. What could I say to that? My guilt felt like a sledge-hammer sitting deep in my gut. "I hear what you're saying," I said to Peaches. "And I promise, I will work on it. I mean that, Sweet Pea," I said seriously, looking over at my second-in-command. "But you"—I turned to JB—"this had better be the end of your Bling Ring days."

"Fine," she said, rolling her eyes. "And I'll give the necklace back to Betty. Of course."

"All of it goes back, JB, not just the necklace."

"Okay, okay," JB said, rolling her eyes. "Even those earrings that Alice never even wears?"

"*Earrings?*" I forced myself to take a deep breath. "They're going back."

Kevin cleared his throat. "You're Joaquin's younger brother?" he asked Ricky, his eyes a little teary.

"Yeah," Ricky said. "Did you know him?"

"We were close friends," Kevin said. "And you know, it sounds like some of this just goes back to the two of you being . . . a little bit lonely? And maybe wanting someone around to look after you?"

"I don't need looking after," Ricky said, defensive. But after a beat, he softened, curious. "But, I mean . . . what are you getting at?"

Kevin shrugged, trying to be casual. "Just that I know

the feeling. Of being left behind. And I know your brother would probably have liked it if I took you for a milk shake once in a while? *If* you promise your stabbing days are over."

"One hundred percent," Ricky said, holding up his hand like he was being sworn in.

"So, what now?" JB asked, handing over the huge stack of cash she and Ricky had nearly absconded with. "Are you guys just going to go back to the game?" JB asked.

Archie scratched his head. "Uh, I kind of feel like maybe we're all over that."

"Yeah." I looked at the other guys. "I don't know about you, but I'm beat. And Dad's on his way, since Dodger and his band of sociopaths pulled a knife." I looked at Dodger. "We might be able to let you out the secret exit, if you promise to scram without any more trouble."

"Are you serious, man?" Reggie asked.

"I am serious," I said. "More than that, I'm tired. Honestly, I don't need to go another round. I'll just give everyone their money back."

"I can get the security system rerouted back to the tablet, if you want," JB offered. "Unlock it all. You guys can walk out the front door."

Dodger glanced at his main flunky. They seemed to be considering the situation.

"The sheriff is coming," I repeated, enunciating my words.

"You pulled a weapon. I'd go now, before we decide we're not gonna be cool about it."

"C'mon, Dodger," the flunky said, fidgeting. "These guys aren't worth it."

"Speak for yourself," Dodger snapped.

To Archie, he just said, "Don't think this is over."

"Oh, it's *definitely* not over," Archie assured him.

"JB, if you'll do the honors with the door locks, I'll escort these losers out of the diner," Reggie said.

"On it," JB replied. She seemed grateful to be using her techno skills for good now. I felt exactly the same way.

"Great," I said, wrapping an arm around her shoulder. "And when that's done, how about we all get upstairs to Pop's? Maybe take one of those milk shakes now? It's been a really long night."

"I don't know if a milk shake's gonna do it, man," Archie said. He tried to smile, to play like he was just kidding. But I could see the haunted look in his eyes. My friend had had a harrowing time. And that was *before* he lost his father. A milk shake wasn't even going to come close.

There was only so much I could say. I clapped a hand on his shoulder, trying to be encouraging. "It's a start."

CHAPTER TWENTY-TWO

BETTY

My eyes peeled open slowly.

I was wet and cold, hands tied behind my back, lashed to a tree.

What's going on?

The dull thud in my skull told me I'd been hit with something, hard—whoever tied me up must have knocked me out—

I remembered, all at once. The woods. The storm. The flitting, floating apparition. Coach Grappler—

Her eyes.

I blinked. At least my eyes were inside my head, for now. Glancing to one side, I realized Veronica had been bound up next to me. "V," I whispered, cautious but urgent. "Come on."

"Ooh. You're up."

I gasped. A figure revealed herself in front of me: tall, twig-slender, swathed in something long and white . . . It was the figure I'd seen dashing through the woods. I hadn't been going crazy (though now going crazy felt like a better alternative to . . . whatever this was).

Up close, she was . . . there was something about her face. Her skin . . .

"Scar tissue," she said, reading the look on my face. "Not very pretty, is it?"

"What happened?" It was Veronica, slowly coming to.

"She knocked us out. Tied us up," I said, frantically trying to piece more of the story together, to determine why this poor girl had grabbed us . . . and what she was planning to do with us now.

"No, I mean . . . were you in a fire?" Veronica's eyes went big, round and full of sympathy. "I had an . . . uncle who'd had an accident like that. I know what burn victims look like. But what happened to you . . . ?" She trailed off.

"What happened to me was unforgivable," the girl finished, seething. "I should have died, truth be told. Sometimes I wish I had, rather than having to live like this—a freak of nature."

"How?" I asked, swallowing. Whatever had happened to her, however it had happened, clearly it had been horrific. The skin on her face was gnarled and twisted, misshapen and textured like tree bark. I could see, too, how the burn pattern traced its way down over her throat, disappearing into the folds of her clothes.

Was her whole body covered in burns? Like Veronica, I had pity for her. But more than that—for as long as she was talking to us, she wasn't *hurting* us. And I wanted to buy more time.

I strained my wrists against the ropes, rubbing the skin raw, but they wouldn't budge. *Crap.*

"*Come join us, Judy,*" she said, her voice a singing lilt. "*Meet us in the woods at midnight.*" Her eyes darkened. "It was a retreat just like this one."

"Judy," I said, panic flooding my chest as I put it together. "You're Judy Johnson. The Stonewall Prep student who went missing here two years ago. The one Stasia told us about."

Her eyes darkened. "*Stasia?* I'm stunned to hear she remembers me." She laughed, a guttural sound that morphed into a howl as she threw back her head. "Has it really been two whole years? I'm not always in my right mind these days. Time tends to go all funny on me. But yes, I suppose that sounds about right."

"And the Baxter High Ravenettes . . . They . . . did something to you? They hurt you?" Veronica spoke slowly, processing the terror of the situation. "They did . . . *this*?"

Judy whirled to us, the melted wax features of her face fixed in fury. "They tied me to a tree, just like I've done to you. Supposedly it was a *joke*; they were going to pretend to burn me at the stake, you see. Of course, I assumed it was just a joke, too. Everyone knows those Greendale girls are witches. We teased them, made cheers about it. Little did we know how poor their sense of humor was."

"So they *lit you on fire?*"

I whipped my head up in the direction the voice had come from.

"Stasia!" Judy cried, looking shocked. "Speak of the devil!"

"Judy," she said, horror creeping over her face as she took in the sight of her former teammate. "There were rumors about what happened that summer . . . that retreat . . . but I couldn't imagine . . ." She trailed off, tears welling in her eyes. "I didn't know."

"You didn't *want* to know," Judy said. "No one did. Not even my parents. That's why it was so easy to disappear."

"You ran away," I said.

"Blondie really is *quite* the super sleuth," Judy said, shooting me a look. "You can imagine how shocked I was to see your little cheerleading squad here this weekend, too, ruining *my* fun—all the more of an issue when I realized just what a snoopy little Nancy Drew wannabe you are."

"*You* sent the invitations?" Stasia asked.

Judy turned to her. "Who else? What better use for my invisibility than to bide my time and plan revenge against the girls who wronged me?"

"The Ravenettes," Veronica said.

"Yes. It was a prank, that's what they said. That Lizzie girl, she wasn't the captain yet—but she didn't stop it from happening, either. If you'll believe it, they were squabbling about the prank—whose fault it was that it had backfired, who was responsible for it going wrong—just as the flames began devouring me alive."

"I . . . don't know what to say. That's unfathomable," Veronica said.

"Yes. Like I said: I should have died. But somehow, I didn't. A storm came—not quite the magnitude of today's storm, but enough to put out the fire. By then, the ropes had burned off the tree, but they had singed to my skin in places. They had to cut it out. The flesh was necrotic by the time I made it to a hospital."

I winced. "And you just . . . vanished?"

"Well, there were months of recuperation, stuck in the hospital as an unrecognizable Jane Doe. But there's no real recovering from such a devastating event. And at the hands of fellow cheerleaders." She shrugged. "I was an easy target, I suppose. A charity case at a prep school with a storied tradition and a family who barely noticed whether I was there. No one wanted me around. Not *really*."

"That's not true, Judy," Stasia protested.

"Isn't it? Do you think the Ravenettes would have singled me out if I hadn't been so obviously vulnerable? So clearly alone?

"After I was out of the woods, medically speaking that is"—she barked out a laugh that sent chills up my spine—"it became clear: I was a monster. There was no place for me in the world anymore. No place that I would have wanted.

"So I ran away," she said. "It's surprisingly easy for girls to vanish these days."

I thought of Polly, disappearing into thin air with the rest of the Farm. I didn't say anything.

"In the end, I'll confess I was surprised that the Baxter High and the Stonewall Prep girls were so easily persuaded back to the scene of the crime," Judy went on, almost trilling now. "I just knew my moment had come. True revenge."

"The Ravenettes, I get. But were you—*are* you really so angry at . . . us?" Stasia's voice was hoarse.

"The Ravenettes were the ones to do *this*—" She gestured at her face, swiping one arm in a wide, angry circle. "But you Stonewall girls? You were supposed to be *my teammates*, my *friends*. You were supposed to have my back."

"I'm sorry!" Stasia cried. "I am! You have to believe me. If . . . if you were watching us, then you know—you know I was keeping my eye on the Ravenettes! I was trying to find out what they did to you, what happened. Being back here . . . the guilt was killing me."

"Too little, too late," Judy said. She reached behind her back and pulled her arm up, revealing a section of metal pipe. Before Stasia could react, Judy had brought the pipe down on her head and knocked her cold. "Better luck next time."

I tried not to react. Things were escalating too quickly now. And with Stasia gone . . .

"Listen," Veronica said to Judy, her voice low and

measured. "I understand why you're upset. You have every right to be— And we can—we can help you!" She was stammering, nervous but working hard not to show it. "We can go with you to talk to the police, whatever you need." Desperation laced her words.

"Yes," Judy laughed, short and bitter. "Because the police are notoriously open-minded toward young female victims who wait several years before reporting a crime." She gave a slow, grotesque wink. "I've definitely seen that on a TV show or two, right?"

"So you were going to . . . what, terrorize the Ravenettes and the Queens all weekend, and then catch some of them? Tie them up in the woods, burn them at the stake the way they did to you?" I flexed my arms again, pushing against the ropes. My wrists were starting to go numb. That wasn't good.

"Aren't you a smarty? Too bad it took you this long to put it all together," Judy said. For a fraction of a second, she really *did* look sorry. "If you'd figured it out sooner, you might have had a better chance of saving yourself."

"And Coach Grappler? Why her?" I asked, panic rising high in my chest.

"She caught me trying to set my little traps. Once she'd seen me, she had to be dealt with. She knew too much."

"So you just . . ." I trailed off, shuddering. I closed my eyes, but I couldn't get the image of Coach Grappler's bloodstained face out of my head. I didn't know if I ever would.

"Judy, listen to me," Veronica said, her voice steady. "We understand how you're feeling. Why you did what you did. Your friends may have abandoned you, but we won't. We're . . . we're on your side. You don't need to *do* this. We're not the Ravenettes *or* the Queens. We can make sure your story is told, is heard. You won't be just another urban legend."

"Look at me," Judy said, practically snarling now. "Do I look like I really care whether you're a *Queen* or a *Ravenette*? Girls, we are long past that point."

My blood ran cold. This girl really was crazy. Not that I blamed her, after everything she'd been through. But still. V and I—we'd survived too much to be taken out here, now. By another *cheerleader*, no less. "You can't burn us," I said. "Not in this storm."

She tilted her head, as if considering this. "Excellent point." She reached into her pocket and pulled out something small and gleaming. She pressed a button and it revealed itself: a long, steel-sharp knife. Its blade was still streaked with blood that I knew was Coach Grappler's. "Good thing I have a pretty effective plan B on hand."

Judy moved closer to me, crouching low, almost feral. She held the knife out, so close to my face I could smell the coppery tinge of the blood. I closed my eyes, bracing for the sensation of the metal slicing at my skin. For an instant, I had a fleeting, irrational thought: Veronica and I, *we'd* be part of this camp's legends, its ghost stories, from now on. This would be our legacy. A fitting end given the sordid details of our respective home lives until now.

Then I heard a crackle, a footstep in the forest, followed by a sharp *twang* that I dimly recognized.

The next thing I heard was a thud, and a piercing shriek from Veronica. The air had changed, too—Judy wasn't looming over me anymore.

Hesitantly, I peeled my eyes open. Judy *was* still in front of me. But she was on the ground now, groaning, the shaft of an arrow peeking through her shoulder, a slow circle of blood spreading from the wound.

"Just in the nick of time, I see," Cheryl said, tossing her red hood back and giving her hair a flip that, were it anyone else, would have been impossible to execute in the rain. "You saved my life, cousin. I'm here to return the favor."

"Cheryl, thank *god,*" Veronica said. "Can you please untie us? I'm officially over giving the great outdoors a chance. This urban sophisticate makes no more apologies. Get me to a hotel suite with room service and a masseuse on call."

"And preferably at least ten percent fewer homicidal stalkers," I put in.

"Understandable," Cheryl said. "Although possibly hard to come by in good old Riverdale. That said, I will commend Camp Sweetwater Pines for its prodigiously stocked archery stable."

"Commend all you want," Veronica said. "As soon as we get

Judy handed off to the police, Betty and I are going straight home."

"They're right behind me," Cheryl said. Sure enough, we heard sirens in the distance, and the flicker of flashing lights. Cheryl glanced at poor Stasia, crumpled on the ground, as she let out a deep groan. "They'll get her the medical attention she needs." She flicked her eyes toward Judy. "Her, too, I guess."

I shivered, thinking again of Coach Grappler's mutilated corpse. "For some people, it's too late."

I tried to shake it off. "Home, huh?" I linked arms with Veronica and, after a minute, Cheryl took my other arm, though not without an enormous, put-upon sigh.

"Frying pan, fire?" I said. I tried to make it sound like a joke, but it wasn't really. And my brain was still a blur of slowly thinning adrenaline, fear, and confusion mixed in with a deep, bone-crushing sense of relief.

"I don't know, B," Veronica said, sighing. "Truly. Maybe there *is* no safe place, not for us. Maybe *we're* the cursed ones. Wherever we go, murder and mayhem seem to follow."

"Are you suggesting that *we're* the common denominator?" Cheryl asked. "I refuse to accept that."

"I'm suggesting that everyone we know has an angle, or a secret, or something they don't present on the surface every day. And that when those secrets rise up, consequences tend to bubble up, too. Painful, nasty consequences."

"But you want to just go home, still?" I said, testing her. I did, too—where else was there to go? What else could we do? The Stonewall Prep girls were still dealing with missing students, possible murders (even if one mysterious disappearance was at long last accounted for). Soon, Jughead might somehow be involved in that, too. I couldn't walk away—wouldn't have even if it were possible.

"I do," Veronica confirmed. "I always will. I guess what I'm saying is that in this case, Riverdale is . . . the devil we know."

"A necessary evil," Cheryl said, echoing the sentiment. "Well said."

I thought about it for a minute. "I can live with that," I said.

The three of us moved forward, pushing through the forest in unison.

I *could* live with that—and I *would*. But for how long?

EPILOGUE

☀ RIVW WEATHER   1 min. ago

Great news, viewers! Our satellites tell us that our severe storm watch has finally passed in full, with only intermittent drizzles expected throughout the rest of the weekend. We may even be seeing some actual sunshine on Sunday night, so break out those shades! Police are still advising citizens to exercise caution on the roads and on your feet, as utilities are working overtime to restore downed power lines and clear fallen trees. Be smart and stay safe, Riverdale!

—RIVW.com and affiliates

ᴧᴧᴧ

Archie:

You're back? Can I see you? Jughead told me—he heard from FP. You sure you guys are OK?

Veronica:

It was a harrowing time, to be sure, but we're home in one piece, and there's nothing I'd like more than some time alone with you. I've aggressively committed to spending the rest of the weekend indoors, in comfort, if that's OK with you.

Archie:

I actually got a *lot* of indoor time this weekend. I'll tell you all about it when I see you. But a night at the Pembrooke sounds great.

Veronica:

I'll tell Smithers to order from Pop's? The usual?

Archie:

Believe it or not, Pop's is closed for the rest of the weekend. Some water damage from the storm. Pop Tate probably just wanted to give you a minute before he filled you in on the details.

Veronica:

All right, see you soon. I'm going to call Papa Ron's. Extra cheese?

Archie:

Perfect. Be there ASAP. Love you.

Veronica:

I'm counting the minutes. Love you, too, Archiekins.

∿∿∿

JUGHEAD

The storm had come and gone, and somehow, we'd made it through, all of us, though some not unscathed. Not by a long shot. Everything was changing for what felt like the umpteenth time, and as we headed into our senior year, having been tested again—collectively, and apart—we felt, in some ineffable way, even stronger. Like our very souls had been fused, forging us into a truly unbreakable unit.

We felt bonded, like with each trauma, each near-death experience (and lord knew, there'd been more than a few of those), our ties to one another had tightened into something stronger than string, stronger than sinew. This was a fact.

But at the same time, paradoxically, things felt uncertain. Untenable. It was like Betty said as they left the forest: *Out of the frying pan, and into the fire.* It was always one or the other. It was never status quo. Never safe. We could never fully exhale.

I wasn't sure, couldn't explain in any rational, articulate terms how those two sensations could coexist so forcefully within me, and yet I knew we all felt the same. I didn't even have to ask; I understood it intrinsically. Betty had told me about the missing girl from Stonewall, and the other legends . . . the other disappearances she may or may not have been linked to.

"Promise me you'll stay safe, Juggie," she said, her eyes wide and searching, as we settled in for a Hitchcock marathon and some much-needed calm *after* the storm.

I kissed her on her forehead. "Of course," I said. Meaning, of course *I'd try.* But *of course,* she had to know: It wasn't a promise I could realistically keep. None of us could.

Riverdale was the devil we knew. That was the other thing the girls had said. The town was a part of us, simultaneously fortifying us even as it rotted us from the inside out. Even as it ate away at our very souls.

All we had was each other. All we could do was keep moving, together, and hope that it was enough.

ABOUT THE AUTHOR

© JDZ Photography

Micol Ostow has written over fifty works for readers of all ages, including projects based on properties like *Buffy the Vampire Slayer*, *Charmed*, and, most recently, *Mean Girls: A Novel*. In addition to writing *Riverdale* novels for Scholastic, Micol is the author of the season three and season four *Riverdale* graphic novels for Archie Comics. She lives in Brooklyn with her husband and two daughters, who are also way too pop culture–obsessed. Visit her online at micolostow.com.